D1177577

THRILLER

THRILLER

AN ANTHOLOGY OF NEW MYSTERY SHORT STORIES BY
**JEFFERY DEAVER • WILLIAM KENT KRUEGER • HEATHER GRAHAM
DON BRUNS • DAVID R. SLAYTON • JENNIFER GRAESER DORNBUSH
NEIL S. PLAKCY • DAHLIA ROSE • RICK BLEIWEISS**

EDITED BY **DON BRUNS**

**BLACK
STONE**
PUBLISHING

Thriller: An Anthology of New Mystery Short Stories © 2023 by Don Bruns
"Wanna Be Startin' Somethin'" © 2023 by Don Bruns. "Baby Be Mine" © 2023 by Kelley Anne Pearson. "The Girl Is Mine" © 2023 by Jennifer Dornbush. "Thriller" © 2023 by Heather Graham Pozzessere. "Beat It" © 2023 by William Krueger. "Billie Jean" © 2023 by Neil Plakcy. "Human Nature" © 2023 by David Slayton. "Pretty Young Thing" © 2023 by Rick Bleiweiss. "The Lady in My Life" © 2023 by Jeffery Deaver
Published in 2023 by Blackstone Publishing
Cover and book design by Kathryn Galloway English

Printed in the United States of America

First edition: 2023
ISBN 979-8-200-84996-3
Fiction / Thrillers / General

Version 1

Blackstone Publishing
31 Mistletoe Rd.
Ashland, OR 97520

www.BlackstonePublishing.com

TABLE OF CONTENTS

"Thriller," in the book world, is a literary genre. So to have the audacity to actually title a mystery book *Thriller* suggests you have some very thrilling stories. I believe, after you read these tales of mystery and suspense, you'll agree that we do. From *NYT* bestselling author Heather Graham, we have the title story, "Thriller." Jeffrey Deaver, author of *The Bone Collector* and the Lincoln Rhyme series, has contributed "The Lady in My Life." William Kent Krueger, a million-selling author, wrote "Beat It," and six other talented, bestselling authors have participated as well.

Our Music and Murder Mystery series continues, following 2022's *Hotel California*. I am amazed at the creativity and devious nature of these writers, and I promise you that you'll be thrilled with these stories. Enjoy!

—Don Bruns

DON
BRUNS

WANNA BE STARTIN' SOMETHIN'

Emilynn Lee through her window could see
The house that was sitting beside her.
The neighbor, though old, *great stories she told,*
Of her life being once an outsider.

What sounded like a nonsensical nursery rhyme was a pretty good presentation of Ruby, the older woman who lived beside her. Emilynn wasn't sure when they'd actually met. Maybe when she walked from the school bus stop several years ago. The lady was walking her dog, and they'd exchanged pleasantries. She and her mother were new to Oakwoods then, the tree-lined street two blocks from Newly Creek.

Then Emilynn was walking her dog on a weekend and the lady asked if she could join her. The fourteen-year-old with Jet, and Ruby with Lady, a cocker spaniel that she named after a cartoon character from the Disney movie *Lady and the Tramp.* Jet was an adopted mutt. Lady, an elegant, *classy broad* Ruby called her. The dogs got along well. Ruby and Emilynn got along well.

The dog walk turned into a regular event, with Ruby asking about the young girl's life, her interests, her hobbies. And Emilynn told her about her poetry, short stories, her love of words and ideas. And she gifted her with a bracelet that she'd made with beads and crystals. When asked, she admitted a love of physical activity. Judo. Her late father had been a sensei. Emilynn worked at the sport and did quite well.

They discussed Kate and Louella, her two best friends, and their dreams and aspirations.

And then, she started asking the woman about *her* past. And the stories were fascinating. At times frightening. A father who was possibly involved in organized crime in Chicago. The young girl didn't really understand the mafia, but Ruby tried to explain it to her. Her father, Sam "Big Sammy" Abrano, as far as the older woman could tell, was a soldier with the Depalma family. Emilynn thought a soldier was someone in the United States Army. There was a lot to digest, and during some of the dog walks, Emilynn wished Ruby would just shut up. She told the young, impressionable girl that she'd been shielded from her father's business as a child, as a girl, but there were rumors of sordid affairs, filled with illegal dealings, and when Ruby talked about a friend of her father being murdered, she asked the older lady to stop.

"I'm sorry, little one." She called her that often. Not in a condescending way, but affectionately. "I seldom have the opportunity to tell my stories, and you are probably too young to hear them."

"Ruby," she said, "I enjoy our conversations, but I'm not even allowed to watch half the movies on Netflix. Yet you tell me stories that keep me up at night." Jet pulled to the left, probably a squirrel, and she tugged on the leash.

Ruby shook her head, the long gray hair softly covering her face for a second.

"Emilynn," she wore a weary smile, looking into the teen's eyes, "life isn't always fair. Growing up, kids were told to stay away from me, my family. The rumors, stories about my father scared people off. I didn't have friends and it was years before I met a guy. I learned in my case that the breaks that happen in life, are few and far between. You are often simply a product of your environment, of the people and situations that surround you. In this case, my father."

And she'd pondered that thought. And, being that it came from someone who was older and presumably wiser than she, she tried to assimilate (her interest in vocabulary coming in to play) the idea, but she couldn't grasp it. She realized at the tender age of fourteen, that you could make your own breaks. Increase their frequency. Not few and far between. And yes her parents were divorced but that didn't color who she was. No. Hell no. She could rise above anyone. Anytime, anywhere.

Ruby had lost her husband at the age of sixty-five. Emilynn had lost her father when she was twelve. Ruby asked her if she had a boyfriend, and the girl frowned, shaking her head.

"How about you?" she asked.

"I use *Over-Fifty*," Ruby said.

"What?"

"It's a dating app. I filled out a questionnaire with likes, dislikes, personal questions, and all kinds of stuff. They match it with men who might have something in common with me."

"And has it worked? Did you find someone?"

"Actually, I think so. We haven't talked but we've emailed a lot. He's a diamond broker out of New York. Apparently doing very well. About my age, and if his picture is real, he's very good-looking."

"Ruby, that's wonderful."

She smiled. "And, little one, he loves dogs."

"Well, he checks all the boxes."

"He's dealing with an African cartel, buying a large quantity of diamonds from a mine in Botswana. I don't understand it all, but he offered to let me invest. There's a lot of money to be made in the diamond business."

"So," she felt awkward asking about Ruby's romantic life, "you are thinking about investing with him?" Better than asking about a physical affair.

"I'm intrigued. Very interested, yes."

Emilynn kept her eyes straight ahead, not looking at her friend. In a very quiet voice, she said, "Ruby, be careful. Please."

"I'm at an age where everyone tells me to be careful. Of what I eat, where I go, what drugs I take or don't take. What I need is an adventure. I can take care of myself. Been doing it a long time."

And the walks continued until they didn't. The teen had waited on the sidewalk for almost fifteen minutes on that Saturday morning, her excited black dog darting here and there, to the end of his leash, waiting for Ruby and Lady. And they didn't show. Emilynn thought about knocking on her door but decided to take the walk by herself. As much as she enjoyed the company, she needed a short break.

And the lady didn't show up on Sunday, or Monday after school, Emilynn watching from her bedroom window, sitting at her desk, her computer showing the latest musings and poems she had composed.

One poem about a teacher named Karen Poe.

Karen Poe taught art and craft
I'm not sure if she perfectly fit.
For art is freedom, no fixed design
Miss Poe, it seems, doesn't get it.

She sent it to a file that no one else would ever see. If a friend (or foe) leaked it to the teacher, it wouldn't bode well for the student. A "B" in art? That had never happened before. The lady was not into freeform.

Tuesday, she walked over to the two-story, ivy-covered redbrick home and knocked on the door. Lady barked loudly from inside. She heard a male voice, shouting.

"Stop it, you mangy mutt."

The door opened and a large man was staring at her. Heavyset, balding, dressed in gray sweatpants and a white T-shirt that was certainly one size too small.

"What?"

"I came to see Ruby."

She'd been so surprised at the big man, unshaven, a sheen of perspiration on his face and arms, she'd missed the slogan on his shirt.

I Want A Beer, Not Your Opinion.

Obviously someone with an attitude.

"She's busy. Sleeping. She's not up for company right now."

The young girl nodded.

"And who are you?"

"I'm her . . . friend. And, kid, don't come over here anymore. Okay? She's sick and doesn't need any company right now."

She started to turn and walk away. Surely this wasn't the diamond dealer. Whoever he was he seemed to be watching out for Ruby.

"Maybe I can walk Lady for her?"

"If the bitch needs walking, I'll handle it. We don't need any help."

The man slammed the door and Emilynn stood on the porch for a minute, thinking about knocking again and demanding that she see the lady. She thought better of it and walked back home.

———

At dinner, over oven-baked French bread pizza, she mentioned the confrontation to her mother.

"You know Ruby is probably in her seventies. It's entirely possible that she fell and had some problems, or is sick."

"Mom, she moves better than I do. And she didn't appear sick the last time I saw her."

"Things can happen quickly, especially at her age."

"There must be something we could—"

"If you don't see or hear from her in the next three days, we'll call the police. My good friend Julie Gwinn's neighbor disappeared last year, and Julie called the police. They did what they call a welfare check. A knock on the door, a request to see if the party is safe."

"Was she?"

Her mother shook her head.

"I was just trying to tell you, there's some help out there. I shouldn't have mentioned it."

"Why?"

"The lady was dead."

———

Detective Evan St. Lifer hadn't had his first cup of coffee. Hadn't even picked up his chipped, worn mug with the picture of a cop car on the surface, the faded slogan printed underneath: *My Other Car Is a Police Cruiser.*

His desk phone rang, and he debated getting his morning jolt and letting the call go to voice mail. Couldn't do it, but he wasn't happy about the decision.

"St. Lifer. How can I help you?"

The voice surprised him. Usually it was a bitter divorce, a jealous husband, or a parent whose kid had disappeared. Somebody was missing, and he had to decide whether the case was worth investigating. Maybe the person had stayed too long at Starbucks, or maybe they had dementia and wandered too far away from home, not knowing where home was. This voice sounded very young.

"I haven't seen my older neighbor Ruby for five days. I think something happened to her."

And he dealt with those cases. Elderly, single people. Their regular regimen disrupted.

"Your name?"

"Emilynn. Emilynn Lee."

"Can I ask your age? And Ruby's age?"

"I'm fourteen. I don't know how old Ruby is, but my mother guesses her age at maybe early seventies."

"Why do you think she's missing?"

"Because we walked our two dogs together, every day. Then one day . . ." and the young teen told St. Lifer the story.

"Can I talk to your mother?" Check in with an authoritative figure.

"Why?"

"Because I just want to authenticate the—"

"I am a mature, self-assured teenager. I have a request that you visit Ruby's home and do a welfare check on her. I don't need you to talk to my mother or any other person. I'm the author of this request. Enough said?"

"Enough said," St. Lifer needed his coffee now, more than ever. A smart-ass teenager and a senior citizen. What a way to start off the day.

He took down the pertinent information. Name, Ruby Abrano. Address, 1651 Oakwoods Drive. Redbrick house with ivy and the girl and her mother were next door at 1649. Probably nothing to worry about, but the story about the lady's family background was interesting.

St. Lifer poured himself a cup of the black demon, as close to the top as possible. He walked back to his desk and Jim Morisey looked up from his.

"Evan, that call that just came in?"

"Some teenaged kid, over on Oakwoods. Hasn't seen her neighbor in four or five days. Wants us to do a welfare check on her."

"Standard."

"Maybe. She gave me a story about this lady's family. Mob connection up in Chicago. Her dad was with one of the families. She didn't understand a lot of it."

"Lady is . . ."

"Seventies. She's guessing."

"There would be no reason at this late time in her life for someone to—"

"Unless she knew something. Had been keeping a secret and someone is afraid she might spill it in her advanced years."

"Listen to you. The conspiracy theorist. A mention of the mafia and right away there's suspicion." Morisey laughed. "My guess, she's fallen and she can't get up. She wandered off and will come home wagging her tail behind her."

"Well, my amused friend, there's a new guy at the house. Sounds like an overweight bully. The kid said he wouldn't let her in, wouldn't let her walk the lady's dog. He told her to go home and not come back."

"So we'll stop by. If the guy's there, we'll get a little aggressive. Tell him we want a visual on the lady. It's not like we haven't done this a hundred times before."

"I'd like to think that we won't have to do it one hundred more times, Jim. I feel like maybe it's time to move on."

"I'm a couple years from mandatory, my friend. I am being forced out, to move on."

"Yeah, and you already act like an old-timer."

"I've got the age excuse. You?"

"I've got the divorce, Cara's cheating with a fellow officer, her move to LA and her cat, Cat. We can't stand each other, but the feline is still here."

"I do feel for you, Evan. You should start dating."

"Where the hell am I going to start looking? It's working these hours and going home to Cat and whiskey. There are no women in those pa-rameters."

"Figure it out, Evan. If you don't, you might go before I do."

St. Lifer nodded. He really did need to dial it back. The lack of so-cialization, and especially the obsessive interest in grain alcohol.

"Can you take a break?"

"From this mountain of paperwork? Hell yes."

"You know, James, we've been told since we started this job that everything would eventually be on a computer. No more paperwork, no more file cabinets."

"They told us a lot of things, partner. The future is hard to predict."

"Let's go see Ruby."

———

The young girl answered the door, nodding her head as if expecting them.

"You're Emilynn?"

"And you want to speak to my mother, because you're not sure I'm telling the truth."

"Nothing personal, young lady. The more verifications we get, the stronger the case."

"Mom. They're here."

The lady appeared from a room on the right. An attractive woman, blond hair to her shoulders, a petite figure, and a wry smile on her face. Evan immediately saw the resemblance.

"I'm Alex, Emilynn's mother. She was sure you'd stop here before you visited Ruby."

"She's a bright girl," Morisey said.

"And she's told you everything she knows."

"How long has it been since you've seen your neighbor?" St. Lifer directed the question to the fourteen-year-old.

"Five days."

"And you saw her how often in the last six months?"

"Almost every single day. Dogs have to be walked, and I don't think Lady, her cocker spaniel, has had a walk during the last five days."

"Would you like to come in?" The mother motioned to the living area, a white leather sofa, blue patterned chairs, and a stone coffee table decorating the room.

An invitation almost always led to a more intimate conversation that led to more details, more solid information.

The two detectives sat in the chairs, mother and daughter on the sofa.

"Tell us about the man who answered the door."

Alex looked at her daughter and nodded encouragingly.

"I know Ruby," she said. "She didn't ever talk about having any kids. I never heard her mention relatives. Her mom and father had passed on and as far as I know there were no siblings. So, after her husband died, it seemed like she was just . . . alone."

"And the man?"

"He simply told me he was a friend." The girl shook her head. "He scared me. Like he was able to get very physical. You know, beat somebody up?"

"She'd never mentioned this guy before? A nephew? A friend from her past?"

Emilynn closed her eyes. For seconds. Maybe half a minute.

"Emilynn?"

"There was some guy. She met him on a dating app."

"And?"

"Probably nothing. She'd never met him in person. They emailed each other. She said the picture he sent was of a very good-looking man. He was a dealer in gems. And she said he offered her a chance to invest in a diamond deal. Somewhere in Africa. I didn't understand it all, and I don't think she did either."

St. Lifer looked at Morisey.

"A diamond dealer? Did she give you a name?"

"No. It was just conversation. Like most of our talks. I'd share something, she'd share something. This time she shared that she was exploring this dating app."

"And it was . . ."

"The name of the app?"

St. Lifer nodded.

"*Over-Fifty.*"

"Did you look up the site? Try to find the guy?"

She shook her head.

"No way. Friends have told me that dating apps are dangerous. Hey, I'm not crazy, and I am obviously *not* looking for someone in that age group."

"Smart girl," Morisey said.

"Besides, Mom told me I can't date until I'm . . ."

"Forty," Alex said. Mother and daughter laughed.

"We're going to visit your neighbor and see if Ruby is okay. We'll let you know what is happening, but don't worry. Most of the time, there's a logical explanation."

The girl glanced at her mother.

"Except when there isn't. Mom told me about a wellness checkup where they found someone dead."

"Let's go into this with a positive attitude," St. Lifer smiled.

Alex smiled back. "I never should have told her that story."

———

"That Alex, she's a looker," Morisey commented as they walked toward the ivy-covered house.

"What? A *looker*? Did you really say that? What . . . did you grow up in the twenties?"

"Well, I'm just thinking that if you were ready to date, you might—"

"No, I'm not ready to date and it wouldn't be with someone I met on a case."

"Where else are you going to find someone?"

"Knock on the damn door, Jim. We're here to find out if Ruby is alive and well."

"Hey, Evan, this Ruby is single . . ."

"Shut the hell up." St. Lifer knocked and after a good sixty seconds, an elderly woman answered the door. Five-one, gray-haired, maybe thirty, forty pounds overweight.

"Can I help you?"

"Are you Ruby Abrano?"

"Who wants to know?"

St. Lifer flashed his badge.

"Detectives St. Lifer and Morisey, ma'am. We're just doing a checkup."

"I'm Ruby. What's this all about?"

"A neighbor hadn't seen you in a while and was worried."

"No reason to worry. Tell that neighbor I'm fine. And you might tell them to mind their own business."

"Do you mind if we come in for a moment? Meet the man who is here?"

"Terry? He's not here. Running some errands. He's my . . ."

"Family?" St. Lifer asked.

"Sure. My sister's boy. Thank you for your concern."

"There was a concern about your dog? Is she . . ."

"She's fine. How is this any business of yours?"

"We're just checking up, ma'am. Standard procedure when someone is concerned."

"I'm fine, the dog is fine, and I would appreciate it if you would go away and not bother me again."

And she closed the door with finality.

Morisey looked at St. Lifer.

"Evan, there was something missing."

"What?"

"There was no dog barking. No sign of an animal."

"Her sister's boy?" St. Lifer glanced back at the house. "There was no mention of a sister."

"In fact," Morisey said, "the girl said that Ruby was all alone."

"We don't have any photograph."

"She looked the age."

"Not quite the sweet lady that Emilynn painted her to be."

"But it appears that she's fine." Morisey motioned toward Ruby's house. "We've solved a missing person case. Pretty easy this time, right?"

They walked across the lawn back to Emilynn's house and knocked on the door.

The teenager opened it.

"The lady, Ruby, answered the door," St. Lifer said. "Told us the man who answered was her sister's kid."

Emilynn shook her head. "Ruby was an only child. At least that's what she told me. There was no one to look after her. She worried about that."

St. Lifer nodded.

"We believe you, but we can only do so much. There's really no sign that she's in any danger."

The girl's mother had walked to the door.

"Did you see Lady, the cocker spaniel?"

"No sign of the dog. But we can't issue a search warrant based on a silent animal."

"Ladies," Morisey said, "as far as we can tell, everything is okay."

"But—" Emilynn started to protest.

"Thank you for your time, officers." Alex glanced at her daughter. "If you see anything suspicious, give us a call. But as of now . . ."

"She's in trouble, detective. I know it." Emilynn turned and walked down the hall.

———

"Something really is wrong," St. Lifer said as he pulled out of the driveway.

"Evan, stop."

St. Lifer braked.

"What?"

"A car," Morisey said. "on the far side of the house."

"So?"

"She said the man was out running errands."

"So maybe there are two cars."

"Humor me. Let's run the plates."

Morisey stepped out and walked up to the gray Honda Civic. He pulled out his iPhone and took a picture of the plate.

"Out of state," he said. "New York."

"I got the impression Ruby's been here for a while. If that car was hers, she'd have local tags."

"Run them when we get back to the station."

———

Emilynn Lee through her window could see
The house that was sitting beside her.
The lady and Lady nowhere to be seen

She studied the childish poem, not sure how to finish.

The lady and Lady nowhere to be seen
She wished things were back as they were.

It would have to do. No one else was ever going to see the rhymes. Except Luella and Kate, her two best friends. They knew the story, and after the police visit, the three young ladies played Nancy Drew in her bedroom, conjuring up the teenage detective and thinking about how she would solve the case. *The Case of the Missing Ladies.*

"She answered the door," Emilynn said. "Told them not to bother her, and then kind of slammed it in their faces."

"No dog?"

"No. And because she appeared, seemed healthy, and didn't complain about anything, they said there was nothing more they could do."

"Would you go back?" Luella asked.

"Well, I suppose if she's there, and everything is okay, I should go back and just ask her why we're not walking together."

Kate adjusted a big throw pillow adorned with a photo of British pop star Jonas Blue, printed with the slogan "They don't speak our language." She and Luella on the bed with the soft champagne-colored spread, Emilynn sitting cross legged on the floor.

"Seriously, girlfriend. If the police won't help, what are you supposed to do." Kate shrugged her shoulders.

"Rely on your help?"

"What are *we* supposed to do?"

"You're right," Emilynn said. "I need to go over and talk to her. Things just don't seem right, and unless she's been lying to me, she's in trouble."

"Why would she lie to you?"

"Maybe she exaggerates. About her family and the mafia? I don't think she was making that up, but I can't be sure. So maybe she does have a sister. And the sister has a son. And maybe she really didn't meet a gem dealer online. I mean," she paused, standing up and staring out the window at the ivy-covered house next door, "I mean . . ." She paused again and her mouth fell open.

"What, Em?"

"There they are." The girl seemed hypnotized. "There they are."

"Who?"

"The big guy and some older lady standing just outside the front door."

The two friends crowded in front of the window.

"Be a great time to confront them."

Emilynn stayed focused.

"That's not Ruby."

"Who is it?" Kate asked.

"It's a lady who isn't Ruby."

"Another lady." Luella smiled. "How many ladies are in this story?"

"Apparently more than two. We aren't done with this story yet."

"Em." Kate spoke softly. "If you go over there now, what if they've, you know . . ."

"What?"

"I don't want to say it."

"Say it. Say it."

"What if they've killed her? And the dog?" Luella closed her eyes.

"Why would you even think that? Say that, Lu?"

"Well, you haven't seen them in how many days, and . . ."

"Just shut up. Okay? I'm going over to see what's going on."

The girl stood up and walked out of the bedroom, her footsteps pounding down the stairs.

She knew Luella and Kate were watching the tableau. The odd-looking couple next door, talking and gesturing on the front lawn. Then Emilynn walking into the scene, seemingly self-assured, talking to the duo with her hands. She glanced back at her house, through the branches of a tall oak tree, directly at the second-story bedroom window, knowing her friends were watching, recording in their minds what happened. She needed their support. You could be strong, confident, and positive about the outcome, but it was easier with some backing.

Pointing to the house, she asked the man, "Where is Ruby?"

He shook his head and motioned to the heavy-set lady.

"Ruby is . . ."

Hesitating.

"Ruby is resting. She's had a rough time of it."

And Emilynn decided she'd had enough.

"Ruby is a friend of mine. I want to know what's happened to her and to Lady. If you don't let me see her, I'll—"

"You'll what? Call the cops?" She shook her head. "Seems you've already done that."

The lady put her arm around Emilynn's neck and nodded.

"Come with me," she said. "I'll take you to Ruby."

Motioning to the man she said, "Terry, I'm going to take this young lady to see our Ruby."

He looked at Emilynn, then at the woman.

"Just take care of things, okay."

"I'll take care of everything, don't you worry."

She escorted the young girl through the front door and the teenager wondered what taking care of things meant. She thought about Kate's comment, suggesting it was possible Ruby and Lady had been killed. And as she followed the mysterious gray-haired woman into the home, she thought about the only person Ruby had ever talked about, the only intimate relationship she'd ever mentioned other than her dead husband. A bond with a person she'd never met, never conversed with. One who flirted with her online. A gem dealer who, by email, invited her to buy into a diamond deal.

———

"Hey, Jim. We got a lead on the guy who walked away from Plymouth Harbor." St. Lifer took a swallow of his hot, black coffee.

"Roscoe Griffith?"

"The same. Walked out of the retirement home and they haven't seen him in a week. Seems he found Speakeasy's on Fourteenth, and as long as he buys the people at the bar drinks and spins preposterous stories during happy hour, the owner has been putting him up in the room upstairs."

"Guy is what? Ninety-eight? Probably having the time of his life."

"Jim, I know we've got more important cases to consider, but that meeting with the woman Ruby? What did you get back on the plates?"

"Car belongs to a Betty Grange. Rochester New York. She's fifty-two, single, and no mention of employment."

"Jim." St. Lifer walked to Morisey's desk. "The girl encountered a large man. The surly woman we met was not the sweet, giving Ruby we were expecting. Probably this Betty Grange. No dog or sign of a dog. And Ruby told the Lee girl that she had no relatives. Yet this Ruby we met tells *us* she has a sister and a nephew. The big guy."

"Someone is lying."

"Exactly." St. Lifer said.

"Who? The girl? To what end?" Morisey stood up and pointed to his computer screen. "Here's the list, Evan. Look, we've got this Ruby telling us one thing, the teenager another, we've got the guy saying he's taking care of Ruby, and then there's the mom, Alex who just shrugs her shoulders. She doesn't seem to be worried."

"Alex, the *looker*?"

"Yeah, I know. I'm old." He smiled. "I understand your frustration. Everyone has a different story, but we can only go so far. It all seems to have checked out."

"You got time to take a break?"

"I don't like where this is going," Morisey said.

"I ran up a history of the Abrano family."

"Ruby's family."

"Her father, Sam Abrano was a thug. He didn't do a lot during his career, but there is a rumor that he was compensated very well. May have put the bite on a group of companies that distributed linen to restaurants in Manhattan. Took kickbacks from a company that sold seafood and steaks to the same food establishments. You know, typical organized crime schemes. But supposedly he had some serious cash when he passed away."

"And?"

"My guess is that Ruby inherited a large amount of that money. Either legally or illegally."

"So, she's rich."

"So, she meets this guy online, and he talks about a deal involving diamonds."

"I see where you're going."

"Last year, romance scams reported over $304 million dollars stolen. You can look it up."

"Now there's a name for this? Romance scams."

"The guess is, it's really double that number but the victims . . ."

"Are embarrassed to admit they were duped."

"Bingo," St. Lifer said.

"With no proof of that happening, with our welfare check completed," Morisey threw his hands up, "what good is there in going back?"

"There was a grainy photo of the family. Sammy, Ruby, and mom."

"And?"

"Ruby was probably fourteen, fifteen. Doesn't look anything like the Ruby we met."

"People change a lot between fourteen and seventy, my friend."

"She was tall, skinny. The lady we met was short and heavy. I think it's that Betty who owns the car. We missed something, Jim. I'd like to find it."

"We're going back, right?"

"We are," said St. Lifer. "We are."

Just then the desk phone rang.

———

"So Ruby is here? Sick? In bed?"

The lady tightened her grip on Emilynn's neck.

"Listen you little twit. You sent the cops over here. We don't need the aggravation."

She squeezed and pushed the young girl through the house.

"She's not here?"

"Oh, she's here." Squeezing harder.

"Stop. Right now. You're hurting me."

"You want to see Ruby? Shut up and keep moving."

And she did. Wanting to see Ruby and find out the truth. Struggling with the choke hold and hoping her friend Kate wasn't right. That the male and female duo had killed Ruby and Lady. The two reached the kitchen, and the lady opened a door.

"Downstairs, twit. Move."

She'd never been inside the lady's home. Never been invited. Their relationship existed outside, with the dogs, the neighborhood, and the casual conversation. Now, she felt like an intruder. She hadn't been invited; she'd been pushed into this environment.

Emilynn stumbled down the steep stairs, grasping the railing on her right. The gray-haired lady was right behind her, arm around her neck.

"You want to start something? You want to call the police and try to upset our little business?"

"I was worried about a friend. I don't know what your business—"

"Ruby says otherwise. She said she told you, and you would probably bring down law enforcement on me and Terry."

"Please. Tell me what business she told me about." The girl shook her head, trying to dislodge the strangling arm.

"Hold still, little girl. You ain't goin' nowhere."

"What did she tell you?" Now a firm, solid question.

"Don't play coy with me. She told you about Terry. That he was a diamond dealer."

"Terry?"

"Terry. He asked her if she wanted to invest one-hundred thousand dollars. And she agreed. Please, don't insult me by telling me that she didn't tell you that."

The teenager said nothing.

"We've offered Ruby the chance of a lifetime, a chance to make a fortune and you go and call the cops?"

"I was worried about her. What do you want me to do?"

"What I want you to do"—the woman held on to her "is to tell her it's in her best interest to give us the money. She's all of a sudden become somewhat reluctant to write the check."

"I can't make her give you the money."

"Oh, but she likes you. She says you share everything and I'm pretty sure if she thought something might happen to you . . ."

And as they reached the foot of the stairs, Emilynn looked up and there, on a worn, gray cloth couch was Ruby. She had on a loose house dress that looked soiled, her hair matted in tangles, and her legs and wrists wrapped tightly with rope. Even in the dim light, the girl could see Ruby's red eyes, probably from crying. An angry welt across her cheek spoke to physical abuse. Across the room was a steel cage. Lady cowered in the corner. She softly whined when she saw Emilynn.

"I'm sorry, Little One. I didn't mean to drag you into this."

"You used her. Said she'd report you missing. You threatened us with this little twit."

A door slammed upstairs, and the big man, Terry, pounded down the steps.

"I told you to stay up there and keep an eye out."

"You've got the papers?"

"Yes, Terry."

"Look, Ruby." He pointed his finger at her. "The sooner you sign these, the sooner you and your mutt can go back to your normal life."

"You won't hurt Emilynn."

"Sign the papers, bitch. As soon as it all clears, everybody is free."

The woman released her headlock on the teenager, and Emilynn messaged her neck and walked to the metal cage, leaning down and placing her hand against the bars. Lady scooted across the floor, then licked her fingers.

"An old lady, a dog, and a teenager." The young girl turned and stared daggers at them. "I hope you're proud of yourselves."

"It doesn't have to get rough. After all, it's only money. Right Ruby?" She turned to the woman on the couch. "The lady has a healthy bank account. We just want a share."

There was a loud pounding upstairs and Terry walked to the steps.

"I told you. You should have stayed up there."

"Yeah, yeah."

The pounding continued.

The fourteen-year-old reached the slip-latch on the cage door and eased it open.

The pounding was followed by loud voices.

With a low growl, Lady leaped from the open cage, barking loudly and bounding past Terry and the lady. She tore up the stairs and the woofing continued.

"You little bitch." The old lady stepped back to Emilynn and raised her hand. The girl kicked out, landing a foot to the knee and the short woman went down, howling and grabbing her leg.

She heard the voices, even louder, shouting her name. Two of them.

"Emilynn. Emilynn."

As the short woman struggled to stand, Emilynn brushed by her, approached Terry, and with a hefty shove, pushed her right hand up under his nose, pressing strongly and breaking the cartilage. Blood spurted as she slipped by him and sprinted up the stairs.

The two men stood there, backed off by the baying hound. St. Lifer saw her and raised his right hand.

"Call off the dog."

And she did.

"Lady."

The dog stopped and stepped beside the teen.

"They've got Ruby tied up downstairs," she said.

"We're on it," said Morisey as he drew his gun and cautiously walked down the stairs.

"There's an old lady with a bad knee, and an overweight guy with a broken nose. If that helps," she shouted down the stairwell. "And Ruby, on the couch. She's been through a lot."

"Your friend Kate called the station. Said she'd watched you come into this house and never saw you leave," St. Lifer said.

"Thank goodness for friends," Emilynn said. "Thank goodness for friends."

———

"Wanted in three states for fraud, kidnapping, embezzlement, and attempted murder." Morisey stared at his computer screen. "Big score, my friend."

St. Lifer studied the papers in front of him.

"Romance scams. It's amazing what people will do for the promise of some companionship."

"Yeah, and it's amazing what a tenacious teenager can uncover."

———

Emilynn Lee, from her window could see
The house that was next to her own.

She looked out the window, and there was Ruby and Lady, looking up at that very window. She put down her tablet and walked down the stairs calling, "Jet. Time for a walk."

DAHLIA ROSE

BABY BE MINE

"Shadow, are you on comms?"

The voice came through her left earpiece making her sigh.

"I'm not supposed to be, in case there's someone scanning for radio waves and you would lead them right to me," she said not so sweetly and through gritted teeth.

The laugh came next. "You know my tech is on point."

"Ego much?" Shadow drawled.

"Reality, babe, just all reality," he boasted. "Any sign of the target?"

"If there was, I would be home with a glass of wine in my hand, soaking in a tub of hot water, soap, and bubbles, and my phones would be on silent," she muttered.

"Sounds sexy, I have a mental image . . ."

"Don't make me shoot you, Grimes. I can turn this gun toward the van just as easy."

"And you never miss a mark," he said in amusement.

He was damn right, she never missed a shot and she left any of her ops like a breeze through the trees. That's why they called her Shadow, out in the open, in the city, anywhere she worked, there was no sign of her after the job was done. Right now she was on top of some seven-story nondescript building that served as a free community clinic and a few other businesses. Not a place that anyone had an interest in the roof, well unless maintenance needed to work up there. Even so Shadow knew it would be easy to hide and keep out of their way.

Hell, she would tinker with the AC or heating units so no one had to come up to the roof so she could get the job done and go home. She hated the city, Fort Jackson, and her house seemed much too far away since she left six weeks ago. Being based out of Fort Hamilton in Staten Island until this op was over was not fun. *Should've been over three weeks ago*, she thought in irritation, but bad guys never played by anyone's timetable but their own. Luckily the air was cooler this time of year, fall in New York came in right after Labor Day. Her ghillie suit did two things, keep her warm and hid her from any view overhead.

Shadow had a camouflage suit for every occasion, her version of a little black dress. She made them herself. She had no trust in the ones provided by her handlers and sometimes she was in that perch for seventy-two hours at a time. So far Grimes hadn't picked up any chatter about a suspicious character on the roof. Her break was coming up, so Shadow could catch a few hours to sleep. Grimes would stay on watch, and she would be at the empty set of offices right beneath her. They paid four months rent on the unit so she could use it as needed, and Shadow had all her gear stored down below. If she needed to book it, she could be gone in less than five minutes.

"No signs of drones or anything?" Shadow asked Grimes, who monitored everything from a van farther down the block.

Grimes blew out a breath of frustration. "None, I'm starting to wonder about Overwatch's intel."

"Seemed solid enough," Shadow said. "Her little boo-thing is still hiding out on this block, and she knows where he is. Those *Baby, Be Mine* gifts come in frequent enough."

"I wonder why he doesn't hightail it to somewhere else," Grimes murmured.

Shadow knew why: he was tired of running and this would be his end game. Instead of that explanation, her answer was, "Who knows."

"I mean who gets involved with a woman like the Dame?" Grimes muttered around whatever he was shoving in his mouth.

"I doubt he knew who she was until shit got real," Shadow replied. "She has a way with men, and they always end up dead."

Maybe he hoped to get her nabbed by the cops or FBI so he could join WITSEC and turn states' evidence. Shadow knew even from prison her target would find a way to have him killed, because if she couldn't have him no one would. Unfortunately, Shadow used the Dame's ex-boyfriend as bait. He didn't even know it, and it was only because she knew the Dame's pattern when it came to men. *I've studied this bitch long enough to know when she takes a pee.*

La dama de las serpientes, the Dame of Serpents would keep coming for this guy. For Shadow to end this, the end of the snake had to be removed, the Dame had to die. She never relished her kills, and in her time as one of the best snipers the army ever trained, Shadow knew her record was pristine. But the Dame, Carina Parez—for all she'd done, Shadow would enjoy putting a bullet through her head.

"Hey, you there?" Grimes's voice broke through her internal dialogue. "Our guy just left."

"He won't be back tonight. I can take a break, eat and sleep, while you keep watch," Shadow replied.

"Yeah I got it covered. When Overwatch checks in I'll give them an update," Grimes answered.

"I got some hot food up there, so you don't have to survive off MRE's."

"I wasn't planning on that crap, not in New York," Shadow said amused. "But thanks for the food, saves me from having to hit the Chinese place down the block."

"You're welcome," Grimes said.

"Shadow going dark, if there's an emergency you know what to do," she said and removed the earpiece from her ear.

With the all clear, Shadow stood and stretched to ease the tense muscles in her back and arms. Staying in one position for hours at a time made her stiff, and for a moment Shadow wondered if this job stunted her from growing or compressing the disks in her back. At five three, she was shorter than her counterparts by far; she smiled knowing she made a smaller target as well. She took the base off her baby, the Barrett M107A1, a .50-caliber sniper rifle, which was an extension of herself. Shadow treated it with extra care, because it could be the one thing between life and death. After moving through the door that led from the roof to a flight of stairs, she opened the emergency exit that would lead to the second floor.

The doors to the offices were locked to any outsiders, and with a sigh, the ghillie suit was removed and dropped near her supplies. This floor was meant to be some kind of medical rehabilitation center so there was an actual working whirlpool in one of the inner rooms. That was her saving grace for the past few months and in less than ten minutes she was soaking her sore muscles and almost asleep in the large metal tub while the jets bubbled the water around her. Back in the area she used to rest, she changed into civilian clothes, and opened the hot bag to pull out two Styrofoam food containers.

"Not fish and his rabbit food," Shadow muttered looking down at steamed salmon with grilled vegetables and a salad. "How am I supposed to survive on this crap?"

A trip outside would be warranted, but not for Chinese food. After seeing what Grimes considered a meal, she wanted a steak done medium rare, a fully loaded potato with all the fixings, mushrooms, and onions. Her stomach growled and Shadow shoved her feet into her shoes grumbling about Grimes and his eating habits. The elevator took her down to street level, when she stepped out into the cool night, Shadow was civilian again, a young woman on the streets of New York. The Chinese restaurant was on the right and she ambled past with the pub on the corner in her sight. Ordering from the corner of the bar, she sat on the stool waiting for them to bring out her to-go meal and enjoyed the music, and sipped a cold beer while she waited.

"Order for Christian Matthews."

"Let me go look," the girl handling the to-go orders said.

The voice made her turn her face away and her heart started to race.

Fuck! He was supposed to be gone for the night, and he was like clock-work. Christian Matthews usually worked at the soup kitchen with the underprivileged at night and stayed inside during the day.

"Hey."

She pretended not to hear him over the music, and he spoke again.

"Excuse me, but do I know you from somewhere?" he said and gave a small grin. "I know it sounds like a pickup line, but honestly you look familiar."

Shadow turned with a sigh. "I don't think so, no."

He stared at her silently for more than a few moments and she shifted uncomfortably.

"What?" she finally asked.

"You are stunning," he finally said, cleared his throat, and then gave a small laugh. "Sorry, that wasn't a pickup line either, just the truth."

She smiled. "Thanks, I suppose."

He chuckled. "I'm never this forward, but you definitely stand out in a crowd."

"And here I was trying to blend in," she said it like a joke, but it was the truth. Maybe she should have eaten Grimes's nasty food and went to sleep. The smell of the pub food coming out for the other guests squashed that thought.

"Christian Matthews," he held out his hand.

She hesitated before taking it and his large warm hand wrapped around her fingers. "S-Shana Brathwaite."

"Very European surname, are you from across the pond," he teased.

Shana shook her head. "Nope, born in the U-S-of-A, but it's a family name from way back, in the Caribbean."

"I was right about the European connection," he smiled, the wait-ress came back with his order and he paid before taking the bag. "Well, back to the salt mines for me, Miss Shana Brathwaite. I hope to see you around."

"Have a great night," she said knowing he wouldn't if the Dame had anything to do with it. She'd have to discuss Grimes's food choices with him so this never happened again.

He gave a small wave from the door, and she let out a slow breath as her food came out of the kitchen and she paid. Shana, a.k.a. Shadow, looked around, making sure there was no sight of him on the street before she walked briskly back to the building and slipped in through the same door in the alley. While Shana ate she thought about Christian Matthews. He had classic good looks, an angular jawline. His eyes were hazel, and his dark hair was cut neatly. Christian was at least a full head, or more, taller than her, if she had stood she wouldn't've reached his shoulder.

In any case, that could not, would not, happen again; she couldn't be associated with the man that would bring the Dame to her. If the worst happened, she wanted no guilt about who he was or what he was. In this job you learned not to make connections. *La dama de las serpientes* taught her that in the most brutal of ways. Shana's hunger was sated and ready to crash for a few hours in her sleeping bag. Before sunrise she would be back on that roof in her position, and no one would tell her she was stunning. *I'm not meant to be,* Shana thought as she washed up in the bathroom that night and brushed her teeth. She studied herself in the mirror wondering what Christian saw in her that made her stand out to him. The only thing that would be known of her would be the precise placement of the bullet from her rifle, and even then, she wouldn't be seen.

———

"Grimes, head on a swivel, I've got movement," Shadow said into her comms piece. "One man walking a large box under his arm, Mercedes driving slow next to him."

"Got it," Grimes answered. "Could they be any more conspicuous as being a getaway car?"

Shadow chuckled. "No one said henchmen had to be smart."

"What's in the box?" Grimes wondered.

"Nothing good," she murmured. "I don't think it's a bomb."

Grime cut in. "Are you sure?"

"Of course I'm not; I don't have X-ray vision," Shadow snapped. "It's not their style though. The Dame likes drama, poison being her favorite. The box has her calling card—*Baby, be mine.*"

"Poison flowers?" Grimes mused. "Diabolical."

The man placed the box on the top step carefully before pressing the button for Christian's apartment and then ran down the steps and into the car. The car drove off at a high speed and from the gingerly way he placed the box, Shadow wondered if it was truly a bomb.

"Grimes, go anonymous and call 911 and tell them it's a possible bomb," Shadow said. "God knows I don't need this to be something that can hurt people walking by, or in the building. Get me Matthew's cell number."

"Is that wise?" Grimes asked dubiously. "I mean would she try to kill him now?"

"Yes, that's why we're here, remember? He's refused all her advances," Shadow replied. "She's losing patience and amping up her game."

"Still, Overwatch said no contact . . ."

"Grimes, get me the fucking number. I'll take the hit if the boss has any issues," she snapped.

"Jeez, okay. I sent it to your burner," Grimes muttered.

If this was Carina's last move to gain checkmate, Shadow would have to start the hunt all over again. The Dame would leave New York to head back to her compound. God knows Shadow didn't want her to go back to Costa Rica, but she damn well would take that woman out one way or another. Her vendetta against the woman was beyond what Overwatch wanted. Her phone was hidden under the ledge by the rifle; she grabbed it and pressed the number quickly, and he answered on the second ring.

"Hello?" Christian's voice was curious, her number would come up unknown so that was to be expected.

"Your bell rang and there is a package outside; don't open it," Shadow said softly.

"Who is this?" Christian's voice became angry, and his next words sounded like they were forced through gritted teeth. "You can tell your bitch mistress, nothing will ever, and I do mean ever . . . change."

"Listen, I have nothing at all to do with the Dame, okay," Shadow said briskly. "But you will die if you don't listen to me. One of her men delivered a large pink box on your doorstep. *Baby, be mine.* Sound familiar?"

"Are you watching me?" Christian asked, his voice stiff. "Are you DEA or something? I don't know one fucking thing about her operation, except that she's a damn killer, and I found out too fucking late."

"You don't have to tell me, we know that you don't know, and I'm trying to protect you," Shadow said. "I know she's a killer, better than most and she'll pay for it. Right now I need you to go downstairs carefully and move that box to the sidewalk. I don't want any of the tenants getting curious about it and taking it in. The police have been called, whatever is in there, don't touch the flowers, don't do a damn thing but put it on the ground and go back up the stairs."

"How long on the police?" Christian asked hesitantly.

"G-man—ETA on the cops?" Shadow said.

"They are already on the way, and from their chatter I'd say about a minute out," Grimes answered.

"Christian, they're almost there," she said. "Are you downstairs yet?"

"Opening the door, where are you watching me from?" he asked. "Can you see me and who is G-man?"

"I can see you," she said looking through her scope and ignoring the second part of his question.

He took each step carefully while carrying the box. "I swear something is moving in this thing. Scorpions maybe?"

"I wouldn't put it past her," Shadow answered. "If they ask: you a have a stalker, nothing more, nothing less."

Shadow turned her attention to her partner in the van. "Grimes, I want video of any onlookers who gather. Carina likes to watch the drama she caused up close and personal, so she's around to see what happens next."

"On it." Grimes's voice came through her earpiece.

"Are you using me as bait?" Christian asked.

"Yes."

"Okay, just wanted to be clear on that," he sighed. "If I'm dead, you can't catch her, can you?"

"Basically."

"You're a talker aren't you?" He gave a small chuckle. "Should I kick the box?"

"No, the cops are here. I'll let them take over," Shadow answered. "Go back to the steps."

"How will I—"

Shadow had already hung up the phone and now she watched the chaos of the police arrival. Christian was wearing gray sweats and a T-shirt stretched across his wide chest. His hands were in the air as the police called out directions to him for their safety and his. He stayed calm throughout.

"I think something's moving in the box," Christian told the police.

"He's not bad-looking. Pretty cool under pressure for a guy being chased by a psychopathic, lovesick drug lord," Grimes commented.

"Probably the thing that drew her to him," Shadow said. "Carina likes them pretty."

"So you think he's hot," Grimes laughed.

"I will shoot you through the side of that van," Shadow warned.

"You don't know where I am," Grimes teased.

"Sitting in the first seat by monitor one, with those chocolate-covered donuts that are going to eventually make you a diabetic right next to you," she told him, and there was silence. "Am I right?"

"Lucky guess," he grumbled.

This time Shadow laughed softly. "Sure, let's call it that and if you ever send me fish and plant clippings for dinner again . . ."

"Yeah, yeah, the same old threat," Grimes said dryly. "It's a salad and it's healthy."

"Says the guy eating donuts like they're going out of style."

"Touché."

Christian was standing behind a cop car and bomb techs in full gear moved toward the box. If was a bomb it would be triggered by lifting the lid. *Unless the Dame has a deadman's trigger, and she's somewhere close watching,* Shadow thought and she used her scope to scan the area. If she spied the Dame in a two-mile radius, depending on the wind, she could take the bitch out. Shadow was one of the few snipers that didn't need a spotter, but she was thirty-two now and exhausted.

The end of the last of her contracts was in a year. She was done then, going into the private sector, and if the government needed her, they could damn well pay out the nose for her services. Shadow focused back on the box and the robot lifted the lid. Nothing happened. One of the bomb techs approached carefully and looked into the box.

"It's just flowers, like a shitload of flowers," he called out, his helmet muffling his voice and he kicked the box over.

"It's not just—" Christian tried to say.

That's when the snakes fell out. All black mambas, seven of them, trying to crawl away from the light and escape. The Dame went for overkill, because the bite of one would do the job. Shadow knew she was still steeped in the religion she perverted; seven was meant to be the Dame's number of power, her immortality. *Not when you meet my fucking bullet, bitch.* In her mind the words were spat out with such malice. It would've shocked Shadow, if she hadn't long made peace with her own savagery when it was needed.

A female cop was on top of the hood of the police cruiser screaming like a bat out of hell—so much so, her hat fell off and her raven black hair fell from beneath it. Shadow only glanced at her quickly through her scope, the cop was facing away from her, fully intent on reaching the top of the car. *It seems like criminals are far less terrifying than snakes.* The police took no chances and before the snakes could slither down a drain, they shot some and the bomb tech managed to use a booted foot to crush two heads. The person bagging them for evidence would have a hell of a cleanup, and Christian was already being put into a cop car. At the police station, Shadow hoped he was prepared to answer hours of questions.

"Snakes. That's stone cold," Grimes made a sound of disgust. "I hate snakes."

"Well, she's done waiting for him to come back to her," Shadow's tone was calm. "Now she wants him dead."

"Hell has no fury like a woman scorned," Grimes said. "Still, I'd prefer to be shot than bitten by snakes."

"She's an I'll-peel-your-skin-from-your-body-until-you-scream-you-love-me type of woman," Shadow explained. "Just make sure you have a background check on any women you plan to bang, so they don't pull a *Fatal Attraction* on you."

Grimes laughed; the sound could only be explained as an old pickup truck on its last leg, but still it made her smile when he laughed.

"What type of woman are you?"

"Grimes, I'm one of the craziest ones you'll ever meet, to choose this as a career," she said with a sigh. "At least I hide it well."

Christian didn't leave for work that night, the cops brought him back home way after he would've left anyway, which meant she wasn't going anywhere either. The other team she had sitting at the soup kitchen was able to take the night off and go get some sleep and some much-needed R&R. Shadow ordered Grimes to do the same. She could handle this alone tonight, and it wasn't like Grimes would be coming out of the van to help her. The bullet that would take the Dame out would be from her rifle, and they wouldn't know where it came from. But Shadow was damn tired of that roof and wanted off this op that had gone on for weeks. She wanted to be free of the hurt, so her brother could finally rest.

Mostly she wanted Carina Perez dead; that was her main mission and her determination would make her sit on that roof for a year to see that happen. When the powers that be put her on the list, because all other efforts to stop her had failed, Shadow made sure that her vast amount of intel on her target ensured her the job. She waited patiently for the sanction to have her killed came through, with no repercussions for killing the vilest woman who was ever created. Shadow connected her earpiece to the phone and pressed Christian's number again. *Hang up*, she told herself firmly, but that order was nixed when he answered the phone.

"Hello?"

Shadow cleared her throat. "Hi, um . . . making sure you're good to go?"

"I thought you were calling to tell me there's another box," Christian said.

"Got my eye on the building—no boxes," she assured him.

"I don't know which is worse, the boxes of doom or the unknown woman watching me," he admitted with a sigh. "This is a shit show."

"I'm part of the good guy crew, and I have your back, unknown or not."

"That's good at least."

She hesitated then spoke. "How did the police interrogation go?"

"Well, I was grilled about who wanted to send me snakes," Christian gave her the rundown. "They played good cop, then bad cop yelled, to help them, help me, the usual jargon. I figured out not much could be done with Carina on my ass like a tick."

Shadow smothered a laugh. "Yeah, thanks for that visual. I couldn't use my resources to get you out: the Dame's reach is long, and she would've heard and gone ghost. I'm sure she has a few cops on the NYPD in her pocket, so you're being out of there and home is a good thing."

"Ah yes, almost forgot I was bait," he murmured.

"Well, I'm glad you're okay. So talk later . . ."

"No, don't hang up," Christian said quickly. "It's been a long few months, and you're the only person I know who hates Carina as much as me."

"How did you get with Carina anyway?" Shadow was curious to know.

"Being a missionary has its pitfalls. She came dressed like one of the girls from the village. She heard about our work and wanted to make sure we weren't DEA," Christian said. "I didn't know that at the time, but she flirted, I reciprocated, and for a while, I thought I was in love. The first time I saw where she lived, I thought, man, she must really help her people in poverty. Wrong. I saw her men kill three of the very same people of her village."

"It's kind of what she does," Shadow remarked dryly. "She's a black widow."

Christian continued his story. "She wanted me to stop my missionary work, to be her boy toy or whatever the heck you are to a drug lord. I said no, and she burned our missionary home to the ground, with women and children inside. We saved most of them, but the other deaths were on me. I knew I had to leave or more people would die, because I was thinking with my dick when I met her. I knew she followed me here when the boxes started. Money, which I gave to charity, threats, poisoned chocolates once."

"How did you know they were poisoned?"

Christian's answer was dry. "Really?"

"Good point." Shadow focused her scope on his building and the surrounding area in a sweep while she spoke. "Well, we knew the basic information of why she was 'on your ass like a tick,' as you put it."

Shadow's scope went back to the window of his apartment. It was dark, and the amber light was almost comforting in a way, his silhouette was an outline and she could see he had his cell up to his ear.

"Move away from the window," Shadow snapped. "If she had a sniper on your ass, you'd be dead."

"Even now, you're watching me." He laughed softly.

"That's the job! Anyway, I have to go."

"Hey, what's your name?" Christian asked.

"They call me Shadow," she answered easily. There was no way he could find information on her even if he tried.

"Why are you looking for Carina?" he asked softly.

"She killed her previous boy toy—my brother."

Shadow hung up the phone and her grip tightened on her weapon as anger flowed through her. When they found Corey he was . . . well, the Dame had torn him apart. She was lucky; Shadow wouldn't be able to give her the same treatment that Corey received. Her death would be from so far away, it would be a whisper in the darkness, and Shadow would have her revenge.

———

The cellophane wrap crinkled as she opened the Pop-Tarts and took a bite of the chocolate breakfast sandwich . . . pastry? How did one classify

Pop-Tarts on a breakfast scale? She had to come to the point of the op where boredom made her think of the most random things. Shadow sat with her back against the wall of one of the empty rooms that were her temporary home. It was her turn to crash and get some shut-eye. After that conversation with Grimes, the meal he dropped off was more to her taste. Grimes was a pescatarian with a sweet tooth. Wasn't that a contradiction to the healthy lifestyle?

Shadow chewed, her mind going from one thought to the next, and then it landed on Christian. Over the next week, they'd talked again—okay, more than once, it was almost twice a day. It felt nice to just have a conversation that had nothing to do with killing or the mission at hand.

"So you like to read and watch movies outside of being a ghost for the military," Christian said. "Are you a drinks and appetizers type of woman or a full meal?"

"Definitely the full meal," she replied. "A beet salad and two scallops is not a meal."

Christian laugh and it was a rich, happy sound that made her smile. "That is oddly specific."

"Because I had it once and it was gross," Shadow said firmly. "My partner likes to torture me with rabbit food, like huge salads stuffed with various lettuces and slivers of carrots, not even any bacon bits. I may have to kill him one day."

"How about you don't do that," he said, amused. "I make a mean steak on the grill. Even better, my stuffed burger with blue cheese and mushrooms will make you think you're in nirvana."

"Is that an offer to cook for me?" she asked.

"Tempted?"

"You never know, I play my cards close to my chest."

Her recollection of their conversation made her smile. With her head leaned against the wall, she took another bite of her tart . . . *Breakfast tart, it's right in the name.* It wasn't wise to get close to the man who was basically the worm on her hook. In her line of work, finding a connection, if any at all was rare, so talking to Christian was unique. Two beeps on her radio made her put in her earpiece: that was Grimes reaching out with their code system for when she wasn't on the roof.

"What's up? Do you see something that looks itchy?" Shadow asked.

"It's not a sweater . . . you know what, never mind," Grimes said. "Your bait is flashing lights at the window."

"Lights like flickering or a flashlight?" she asked with a frown.

"No, like morse code for *call me*," Grimes chuckled. "One might say you have an admirer."

"Suck it, Grimes." Shadow pulled the comms piece from her ear.

She picked up the burner phone and pressed the button to redial his number. It was like the beginning of an addiction, where it was more titillating than anything else. *I've started taking him right to the vein for a better hit, and I'm screwed.* Her thought amused her, and she was chuckling softly as he picked up the phone.

"You actually laugh," Christian said in lieu of hello. "It's a nice sound."

"Don't ever signal like that again," she snapped. "What if someone else saw it and could understand what it meant?"

"Wait, that actually worked?" Christian was amazed. "Shoot, I found it on the internet and used the lamp so it wouldn't look like I was doing it on purpose."

"Well, it did and it's dangerous. If you want to talk to me, wait for me to call. As is, I am breaking all—and I mean all—protocol calling you."

Christian was silent for a moment. "Will you get in trouble for talking to me like this?"

"What my handlers don't know won't hurt them," she softened her tone.

"I hate how that sounds: handlers, like you're some pet in a zoo," his voice was grim.

"It is what it is. I chose this life," she said simply. "So you taught yourself morse code to contact me."

"Impressed?"

"Might be." She gave a soft laugh.

"You have a nice laugh."

"It doesn't happen often, trust me," Shadow said amused. "In my line of work, you don't go home to dinner parties and a group of friends when the op is over."

"Sounds like a very lonely life." Christian's voice held sympathy.

"I manage." She swallowed the lump in her throat, knowing that loneliness swamped her more often than not when she was home.

Christian hesitated before asking. "What about your family, a husband or wife?"

"You're moving. I heard the door slam," she said. "Where are you going?"

"To pick up my dinner from the Chinese place," Christian answered, and his voice was filled with amusement. "You have hearing like a bat, my door doesn't even squeak, and the door didn't close all the way to click."

"I've heard worst things about myself," she said.

"Okay, so back to the question you promptly glossed over, who's waiting for you when this is done?" His footfalls went down the stone steps, and he was wearing sneakers, but if she mentioned it, Shadow knew he would comment on her hearing again.

"None of the three. Parents didn't give a damn, so I was raised by the system. Joined up with the army at eighteen for some place to sleep and eat," Shadow answered bluntly. "I had my brother, but technically he wasn't my brother, we just grew up together in foster care, so we took care of each other."

"At least you had him," Christian said gently.

Till I lost him to the Dame, she thought before speaking. "I found I was proficient at the army stuff, especially guns, and that leads directly to where I am now."

"Ah, a life condensed in less than a paragraph."

"It doesn't pay to get attached. It usually ends badly." Shadow broke off a piece of her second Pop-Tart and popped it into her mouth. "If I ever get burned, anyone who knows me is in danger."

"Burned?"

"If my cover is ever broken and my real name is ever found out," she explained. "Or if the government decides I'm no longer worth being kept hidden and they drop the intel themselves. It's a great way to get rid of a person: just let the enemies they made take them out. Nice and easy with no mess on government hands."

"They wouldn't do that, would they?" Christian sounded outraged.

"It happens, not often, but it does." Shadow didn't even know why she was talking to him like this but it felt good to unload.

"It all makes me feel very punchy," he muttered.

She grinned. "Thanks for the support. You want to punch people out on my behalf?"

"Yes."

"That's sweet." Shadow wouldn't even mention that she could kill just as easily in hand-to-hand combat. It was the first time someone wanted to be her protector; it felt nice.

"You sound like someone I know—well, not know, met," Christian admitted.

Her heart raced. "I'm not usually anywhere for someone to meet, where did you see this woman?"

"At a steak place close by, your voice is husky like hers," Christian laughed softly. "Please don't think that I'm some kind of ladies' man, talking to you and hitting on women all over the city."

"Why do you care what I think?" she managed to say.

"Because I do." It was a simple answer that came easily from his lips.

"What did this woman look like?" Shadow asked.

"Gorgeous, waves of curly hair and skin that was a little darker than teak. She had soulful light brown eyes, and she didn't smile, and her voice was what drew me in," Christian said. "She seemed sad, or maybe tired. I don't know, but I wanted to make her smile, laugh, and see happiness in her eyes."

"I should hang up on you for that very deep description of a woman you just met," Shadow teased huskily. Why did she need to know how he saw her, and why was she happy with how she was perceived? Christian's description made something flutter in her chest.

"I look past everyone's face. The eyes are the windows to the soul,"

Christian sighed. "Unfortunately, I didn't look close enough at Carina's because if I did, I would have seen the devil and the flames of hell."

He was in and out of the restaurant in less than five minutes and even thanked the person behind the counter in mandarin. That added another layer to him. He traveled extensively working for the disaster charity. His dossier was filled with destinations from Haiti to Sudan, so clearly he took his job seriously.

"That's called thinking with the little head," Shadow snorted.

"We're on to the sexy part of getting to know each other, are we?" Christian drawled in amusement.

"We are not getting to know each other," she said dryly.

"Wouldn't you want to know me?"

"The girl in the steak house, remember?" Shadow said softly. "I'm sure you don't want me thinking you're fickle."

"There is a one and a million chance that I will ever see her again," Christian said. "I wanted to comfort her, I think."

"And me?" Shadow asked.

"I think you need that and so much more."

Christian's voice held something . . . She couldn't put her finger on it because she'd never allow herself to recognize what it meant. She was about to respond when her radio made three short beeps and without hesitation, Shadow put her earpiece in and answered Grimes.

"What's moving?" Her tone was all business just as easily as she laughed.

"Two on foot, two in a car, and they're packing hardcore," Grimes said.

"No time for the roof. Shit!" Shadow pulled on her ski mask and then a hoodie as she spoke. "Christian, drop that fucking bag and slip down the alley now. Run!"

"What's going on?" he asked but she could hear him moving fast.

"You've got four coming at you hard . . ." she muttered and then Shadow heard the shots. "Fuck!"

She dropped the burner to the ground, not caring where it landed. "I'm going on foot, Grimes!"

"Let me call the other team—" Grimes began.

"No, if the Dame sees anyone that looks like feds, she's out!" Shadow took the stairs. "I'm covered so there is no way to recognize me. I'm going small arms and hand to hand."

"Fuck me sideways, I hate when you do this," Grimes muttered. "Don't go getting yourself dead—I would hate to train someone new."

"Yeah, yeah, like you actually trained me," she muttered sarcastically, the southern twang coming through. "Where's Christian?"

"Christian is pinned down somewhere. He's not on the street and the car took off with only the driver, so you have three to handle," Grimes said.

"Scramble a cleanup crew; you know the cops are coming. Even in this neighborhood, they'll take their time." Shadow's breath heaved out of her as she took the stairs two at a time. "I want zero chatter on this. Get the crew to shut it down."

"On it."

She stayed away from the streetlights, using the darker portion of the street to slip down to the ally. She put herself against the wall, with a quick glance to see where the Dame's goons were. They were spread out the width of the alley, as if expecting Christian to try to run by, while they move slowly toward the only hiding spot down the dead-end alley, behind the large dumpster. She hoped to God he wasn't in the damn thing, because there aren't enough antibiotics and soap to combat a New York City dumpster.

Shadow knew their focus wasn't on her; she would have to be precise and quick with her plan. The first shot from her handgun was to take out the light and plunge the alley into darkness. That made them all turn, just as one of the gunmen went down with a double tap to the head and chest. She didn't get off another shot, she combat rolled toward the two that were left and pulled the knife from her boot. She finally stopped at a low crouch, Shadow threw the knife with precision, and it lodged into the neck of gunman number two.

She heard a low snarl and Christian came barreling from the side of the dumpster where he hid and tackled asshole number three and began to pummel him in rage. He could fight, Shadow had to give him that. The Dame's goon was on the ground, and Christian was breathing heavily, ragged—all the fight left him as suddenly as it came. She walked over and shot the man in the head, before turning to walk away. Silence rang between them for a moment before Shadow spoke.

"Get going, go to the pub or something, don't come back to the apartment until you hear from me," she told him briskly. "I don't want you around in case the cops come sniffing. We need to make it like this never happened."

"Stop, wait . . . at least let me see your face."

Shadow had just pivoted to leave, and his voice stopped her steps, but she never turned back to him. Instead, she ducked her head lower and kept to the darker area of the alley.

"That's not going to happen, Christian." Her voice husky, Shadow cleared her throat before speaking again. "Go, I'll call you later."

"Carina's going to know I had help here," he pointed out.

"Yeah, I know. Let me think on it," she said, and this time she did leave.

Move with a quickness, that was her trainer's motto, and she lived by it. She was back in her building and up in her nest in less than ten minutes. Through the scope of her rifle, she watched the crew remove bodies. The explanation would be a drive-by or gang initiation; of course, some cop would try to tie it back to Christian. They wouldn't be able to because Grimes would make his alibi airtight if any of New York's finest still decided to sniff around. An idea came to her slowly. It was the best way to get Carina out in the open.

"Grimes, see if the crew took any cell phones off any of those guys, then you track that shit, every number, until it leads me to the Dame."

"What are you planning?" Grimes asked curiously.

"I'm going to make her come to us," Shadow said. "This is going to be over one way or another, and we have to bring Christian in on this."

"Oh boy," Grimes muttered.

"Go big or go home," she said.

It was another two hours before she called Christian's number and give him the all clear to come home. They didn't talk, she would leave that for tomorrow. For now, she would keep watch from the scope of her gun and protect Christian the only way she knew how: killing anyone who tried to take his life. It was much more than just her revenge now, Christian's life was important to her and that may just be her downfall.

———

"So you want me to reach out to Carina and tell her I want to meet her," Christian asked over the phone.

"If you call, she will answer, and show up, because she's not scared of being arrested. Or dying, for that matter," Shadow pointed out. "In her mind, you still belong to her, and you're calling your lover home."

"So not tempting," he muttered.

Shadowed sighed and pinched the bridge of her nose. "For you, no. For her brand of crazy, yes. Her pride will make her come because: How dare you leave her?"

"Isn't that essentially the same as making me walk into a nest of scorpions?" Christian asked skeptically.

"You can handle it. You beat the crap out of one of her men, and I have your back."

"Do you?" Christian's words were clipped. "You wouldn't even show me your face in the alley."

Shadow looked through her scope just as he walked away from the window, and she didn't have to chastise him about making himself a target.

"What would've come from doing that?" Shadow asked.

Christian countered. "I would be able to see who the hell I was trusting with my life."

"I've been watching you for weeks, and I would still be doing it without your knowledge if it wasn't for those snakes," she spat out. "I think you can be sure I have your back. I came out to help you last night."

"Yeah, I saw how you did that," he said. "You killed them without any hesitation. That level of coldness, I wasn't expecting."

"What *did* you expect? Me to talk to them, let them pray before

I shot them?" Shadow took her gun down from the ledge and sat with her back against the concrete.

His reaction hurt because she was trained to be this person, beyond being a woman who loved good wine and wanted something more. At the end of the day, she was a tool to the people who pointed her in the direction of a target and said, "This one." It was her job to make her targets not exist.

"I'm a killer, Christian. I never said otherwise, and it's not romantic. It's not time to think; it's kill or be killed, and I did it so you wouldn't die," she said bluntly.

"Still . . ."

Shadow hit the roof with her folded fist. "Save me your sanctimonious missionary morals, would you? This is why I can't get close to anyone, because of their own perception of who they think I am. I'm no hero. I do the job I'm paid for and play the hand I was dealt. Are you going to do it or not? Do you want this to be over? Do you want your life back?"

"I do," he sighed. "Sorry, I lashed out. I— I'm so sick of this, you know? My life turned upside down by two women: one who wants to kill me and the other protecting me from the shadows. An unknown entity that I know only by her voice."

"Hence my name."

A sad laugh escaped Christian. "I guess so."

"Would you want to know me?" Shadow asked hesitantly.

"Yes," his answer was simple. "There's more to you than being a killer, even if that's what you believe. You may know how to take a man out in several different ways. But then there's an innocence about you that you hide beneath all that badassery."

"I don't know what I should say to that," Shadow admitted.

"How about this," Christian offered a solution. "After this, we get to know each other—no fading off into the sunset, no blending in with the dark like Batman."

"I don't live in New York," she told him. "This was just the destination and after this is over, I leave."

"We'll sort all of that out," Christian said firmly. "Give yourself a chance to find out, to know someone that's not behind the scope of a gun. You can have something outside this job that is filled with death. You deserve to live a good and happy life."

"I've got a year left on my contract, maybe after that . . ."

"Nope. Now." His voice was stubborn. "You need a port in the storm other than going home to an empty house and silence."

"I'll think about it," she told him. "Now make that call and put it on speaker, I need to hear her exact words. I'm assuming you have a personal contact number, or do you need it? All the numbers on her men's cells went dark when they were killed."

"I still know how to reach Carina," Christian answered. "I'd rather have a direct line to Lucifer, but I can reach out to her."

"It may be one and the same. She has to be from the seventh level of hell to do the things she does," Shadow countered.

"Good point," Christian said dryly. "Okay, let's do this, calling now. Wait, how will you hear the conversation if you're not on the line?"

"I'll be able to hear just fine," she said.

"My house is bugged isn't it?"

"Make the call."

He muttered something under his breath before hanging up and she smiled, then she put her coms earpiece in.

"Grimes, the call is being made, so you're on," Shadow said.

"Understood," Grimes was chewing something. "Getting it patched into you now."

"Stop with those donuts," Shadow said in exasperation. "I'd like to have you around for a while."

"Awww, you care."

She snorted. "I just don't want to have to train someone else, I've got a year left on this contract, seems annoying to have to do that now."

"Touché." Grimes laughed. "You know you love me."

"Uh-huh . . . I will admit that ops like this with you and not being in some jungle alone have its merits," Shadow told her partner.

"See, you *do* care . . . my heart just grew three sizes too big."

"That's the heart attack waiting to happen if you don't cut that crap out of your diet, and no, salmon and veggies do not offset your sugar intake." The phone ringing from the call Christian was making came through the devices planted in his apartment. "Now shut it, so I can hear."

Shadow noted that she was holding her breath as the phone rang and forced herself to release a slow breath. The ringing stopped, and there was silence for about thirty seconds before she heard the voice of the Dame. Shadow felt the hair on her arms rise at the voice.

"My Christian, I thought you would never call me," the Dame's voice was cool and her accent thick. "I miss you, my darling. You did not reciprocate any of my gifts."

"*Baby, be mine*—Carina, really?" Christian gave a short laugh. "Are you this delusional that you fooled yourself into thinking I love you? I was never yours, not in the way you want."

"But yet you are calling your beloved," she crooned. "Maybe something got through to you, yes?"

"She's beyond crazy," Grimes said in a low voice. "She really thinks they're a couple."

"A profiler would have a field day with her kind of insanity," Shadow replied. "She's only hearing what she wants to hear, and to her, Christian loves her."

"There are not enough woo-woo pills to cure this one," Grimes replied.

"Hmmm," Shadow made the sound instead of an answer. She was listening closely for any undertone or cues from the Dame, in case she needed to nix the plan she concocted.

"We need to talk face to face, Carina. Alone, no one else. Not your goons or anyone." Christian's voice was like ice. Shadow assumed that was how he needed to speak and lock up the part of him that believed he was in love with a monster.

"What about you, I am sure you did not kill my men alone," Carina laughed softly. "Is it the FBI, or DEA—are they there with you now?"

"No one helped me, Carina. I just got tired of your bullshit and then you send people to kill me?" Christian snapped. "Of course I armed myself and I killed them all."

"I knew you had that fire in you. Imagine how much we could do together." The Dame's voice sounded excited, like thinking of the fact that she'd forced him to kill was arousing.

This bitch was getting off on the thought, Shadow thought incredulously.

"The DEA did come to interview me at the police station after the snake incident," Christian was ad-libbing now, and Shadow frowned as he deviated from the path. "You torture people, killed more, they said the same would happen to me."

"And what did you tell them, my Christian?" The Dame's voice became wary and soft.

"That you wouldn't hurt me," Christian said. "That I left because, while I don't like your lifestyle, I still loved you—and I had not one damn thing to tell them."

"Very, very good, my beloved," the Dame crooned. "I will send a car for you, and we will talk then about you coming home and how you will make up the last few months to me."

"No, Carina, this time it's on my terms, my place. You may love me, but your people hate my guts," Christian said bluntly. "My apartment, tonight at ten, and we settle this once and for all."

There was silence on the other side of the line before the Dame answered. "I'll come to your home, and I will leave my protectors in the car."

"Yes, leave Raphael and Judas in the car," Christian's voice dripped with sarcasm. "A man with the name of an angel and he's a sycophant. At least Judas is named aptly. One day he will sell you out."

The Dame's laugh was light. "Don't be jealous, my love, you will come home and protect me. I will be at your home promptly at ten; make sure the bedsheets are clean."

"I'm not sleeping with you, Carina," Christian said firmly. "We talk before anything else."

She laughed. "You could never resist me, beloved, and you won't now."

Shadow's face wrinkled in disgust, and a tinge of jealousy went through her at the thought of Christian in bed with that woman. She gave it thirty seconds before she called his number, and he answered on the first ring.

"Did you get all of that?" Christian asked in lieu of hello.

"Yep, and the ick factor is high," said Shadow as a shudder of revulsion rolled through her. "I almost caught chlamydia listening to her voice."

"Trust me when I say, I feel just as dirty," Christian agreed.

"Well, she sticks to her pathology of being a sociopath," Shadow explained. "You, her goons, and any male she sets her eyes on is a protector. She wants to be the kitten who is catered to, and when she isn't, then the alley cat that carries a switchblade comes out to play in blood."

"You could not be any more true—she is a vicious bitch and enjoys the torture, both watching it and taking part," Christian added quickly. "I'm sorry if it made you think of what your brother might have suffered."

Shadow spoke silently as the images of her brother's body filtered through her mind. "I saw that in live and living color."

"You know I'm going to kill her right, and her people?" she asked bluntly after a moment of silence on both ends of the line.

"I know."

"Okay," Shadow blew out a breath. "If it goes bad, the office building across the street, alley entranceway, Grimes changed the code to six-six-six-one. You come inside take the stairs to the seventh floor and wait for me."

"Is that where you're positioned?" Christian asked in amazement and his voice became husky. "I could have reached out and touched you all this time."

She laughed. "I would've probably broken your hand and killed you for breaking in."

"I like when you laugh," his tone dropped an octave. "Will you think about us meeting, maybe a date, after this is over?"

"I don't date."

"You should start."

"I'll think about it. I'll be ready at eight," Shadow explained. "I'm going dark, so you won't hear from me until this is over."

"Good luck," Christian said.

"I don't need luck. I never miss."

———

Her finger tapped against the trigger of her gun, not with impatience but with the knowledge that tonight might be the end of her mission. To kill the woman who killed her brother and then maybe she could sleep without seeing his broken body in her dreams. He was her big brother and larger than life. When it came to Carina, Shadow couldn't protect Corey, and the Dame ate him alive. Corey liked the fast life—the money, the luxury, and everything about what Carina had. But then, like Christian, he saw what lurked beneath. Corey came to her for help, to get out and away from the vile and poisonous woman.

But the Dame found out and tortured Corey until he begged for death, then Carina put a bullet through his head. Shadow was graced with picking up his body from the side of the road with a flash drive of his torture, just to prove that no one should dare try to go after the Dame. It only served to be a fire in Shadow's soul to make sure the serpent queen died by her hand, and her finger itched to pull the trigger. She slowed her breathing so her heart wouldn't race, adrenaline led to mistakes, and she wasn't about to make one now.

"We have movement, Shadow." Grimes voice sounded in her ear. "Police car, coming down the block driving slowly."

"The NYPD must still be curious; they'll go by soon enough, when they see all is quiet," Shadow said. "Shit, they are stopping."

"One male, one female cop, brunette woman. Isn't that . . ."

"The cop on the car when the snakes tried to slither away?" Shadow said in amusement. "Yeah."

Shadow used the scope to look closer. "They're ringing his doorbell. Damn it, it's almost ten o'clock, and our target will be here in minutes."

"The wire is picking up the conversation," Grimes said. "Let me get you tapped in . . . holy shit."

"What?" Shadow said quickly, a cold chill coursed down her body when she heard the conversation.

"Carina, you had some work done," Christian's voice was calm.

The Dame laughed. "Not really; I decided to go back to my natural color. I have someone with very good skills at makeup and, what are they called, prosthetic feature things . . . effect artist?"

The Dame was the cop . . . she was so close that they didn't even catch it. Shadow's mind started to race.

"The cop with her, is he legit? Grab a shot of his face, while he's standing there and run it," Shadow demanded.

"On it," Grime's fingers worked his magic, and she could hear him tapping furiously on the keyboard. "Adam Holden, ten years on the force. That's confirmation she has cops in her pocket, that's for s ure."

"Send all you find anonymously to the One Police Plaza," Shadow tried to focus on the conversation. "I need to figure out a way that Christian can get her outside."

"So you had a makeup artist do this just to get close to me, and you were on the cop car screaming your head off at the snakes," Christian was speaking again.

"I am also a very good actress," she said and laughed lightly. "Now, don't try to run, Christian. I have my Raphael and Judas at the back door. Not very smart taking the bottom floor apartment."

"I thought it was the perfect apartment with a quick escape. I was apparently wrong," Christian answered.

"Let's go inside and talk, shall we?" The cop pushed Christian ahead and Carina followed.

"Why won't you leave me alone, Carina? You can have anyone. Why me?" he asked.

"But I want you, *mi corazon,*" the Dame crooned. "You are my love, my Christian, and if I can't have you, why would any other woman ever get to taste your lips?"

"Because that's how breakups work, you go your way and I go mine," he protested.

"No one leaves me," the Dame snapped. "You come with me to-night, darling, or I taste your last breath on my lips."

"I don't want you!" The exasperation in his voice was clear. "God, why don't you get it through your head?"

"Why can't you get it through *your* head that no one leaves me!" the Dame screamed in anger. "I deserve love too; I deserve to be happy."

"You do, Carina," Christian said softly. "But you need help, because everything you do is completely evil. People are your toys! You claim to love me, but you're willing to kill me."

As the conversation went on, Shadow trained her scope on the window, hoping she could get a good shot. The Dame was smart and, though she could see their silhouettes, there was no way to make sure her bullet would meet its target and that pissed her off.

"Grimes, get the other team to roll with blue lights up on the street at the back of the building. I want them to go in heavy, guns drawn and with their vests, all the pomp, and pageantry of a full-on raid. That will get them moving inside, she'll try to escape through the front."

"Team two, target on site. We need to get the targets to be on the move," Grimes said. "Roll up on Martin Avenue with all the pizzazz."

"Copy that; team two on the move," came the scratching reply on the comms.

"What about the cop in the front door?" Grimes asked.

"That's where you come in," Shadow said grimly. "Make a little noise, get him to come to you, and I'll do the rest."

Shadow watched through the scope as Grimes unfolded himself from the open sliding door of the van. You would think he would be this over-weight guy who needed sun and exercise, but Grimes was tall and built like a Mack truck. That's why he ate so much, because he burned through calories like it was wildfire through kindling. Their constant sparring about his eating habits kept them entertained on long ops, and sometimes it came in handy, because Grimes bent over and happened to drop a syringe.

"Help me," Grimes groaned and dropped to his knees. "Diabetic . . ."

A woman passed by and stopped, waving to the cop at Christian's front door. "Hey, Officer! Officer, we need help!"

Shadow saw him look at Christian's door and then with a sigh jogged toward where Grimes was playing it up.

"You can go, ma'am, I have this covered," the officer said to the woman. "Thank you for getting my attention."

She walked off, looking back once then twice to where the police officer was bent over Grimes.

"Get up, you idiot, I have zero time to be fucking around with you and your damn diabetes," the cop said angrily. "You have a fucking box of donuts in your hand, what did you think would happen?"

"This." Grimes said and in seconds he had the cop incapacitated and dragged into the van. "I'll tie him up all pretty for his boys in blue. You're up, Shadow."

Her finger was a feather-light caress on the trigger as she waited to fire. Shadow hoped the NYPD threw that cop, and anyone else who went against their oath, in jail. The operation picked up speed after that, the blue lights bouncing off the wall of the alley and the sound of bullets ricocheting off brick walls filled the air.

"We have to go!" She heard one of Carina's men's voices and it was urgent. "Let me kill this fool and go!"

"The hell you will!"

Christian snarled, and Shadow hated the fact that she wasn't in there with him—instead she had to listen through some damn bug in his apartment. There was a cry and then the sound of a fight. *Jesus, were they killing him?* Shadow was about to put everything she was taught into saving him when a scream of rage from the Dame came and Christian spoke again.

"I will let her go when I'm safe!"

"Kill him," the Dame screeched. "Kill him now!"

A shot was fired but she breathed out a sigh of relief when she saw Christian's door open, and he backed out holding on to the Dame's struggling body. When he was on the top step, he pushed her back inside and turned on his heels to run, there was blood trickling down the side of his face and then coming through his fingers as he held his upper arm. The shot must have grazed him, and it looked like he gave as good as he got in the initial fight. Christian looked up at the roof of the building before he started to jog across the street.

"Come to me, baby," Shadow murmured, noting the term of endearment she used—now was not the time to think about that—as she looked through the scope. "That's it, do exactly what I told you."

Christian was lost to her gaze when he crossed out of sight and into the alley and Shadow never moved her focus from the front door. The second team wouldn't enter, they knew that there was a black tag on her, and Shadow's mission was to kill the Dame. They would sure make it seem like they were coming in, though, and when the first of Carina's men came through the door of Christian's apartment, Shadow held her breath.

All three need to be outside for her to do her job, and seeing their companion gone was the push they needed. They flanked the Dame as she went down the steps, her now brunette hair wild from the fight and being held as a shield. They weren't thinking about Christian anymore, only about escape because they were cornered. Shadows first bullet took out the man to the left and her second "protector" fired wildly. In rapid succession Shadow took him down as well. As if accepting her fate, Carina, the Dame, opened her arms wide and Shadow watched her lips move.

"The angels will protect me, the angels will guide me," Carina called out loudly.

"God won't have you," Shadow replied to no one but herself.

The bullet left the gun, and it was as if Shadow could see the path as it went through the air and then it connected with the center of Carina's head. Surprise bloomed on her face before she crumbled to the ground.

Shadow cleared the metal cartridge from her gun and slipped it into her pocket. "I hope the angels drag you to hell."

Shadow took her gun off the base and as she efficiently packed up her gear, she spoke over comms, "Grimes, pull the team. Target is terminated, time to jet."

"Your ride is parked," Grimes replied. "Nice doing business with you, as always, Shadow—till we meet again."

"In a few months," Shadow smiled. "Take that guy and drop him off at the plaza, I'm sure they want to talk to their officer," Shadow said.

"On it," Grimes said. "Tell Christian I said hey and, Shana . . ."

"What?"

Grimes very rarely used her real name.

"Take the guy home and try to glean some happiness out of this life," Grimes said gently. "We have a dirty job, lots of death. I have Deb and the girls . . . even if they don't know what I do. Get yourself a port in the storm, someone to come home to."

"See you in a few months," she replied tersely.

Grimes chuckled. "Later, Shadow."

She pulled the comm from her ear and ran down the stairs. It was imperative that she fade into the shadows before the cops, then DEA arrived. What would she do about Christian? Grimes advice seemed plausible, and when she opened the door to the empty business suite, Christian was standing there. Shadow hadn't been close to him since that night when she was picking up her food. Being this close to him, knowing him better, her heart began to beat faster.

"I'm taking it you're my silent hero?" Christian's voice as a deep timber.

"That's me," she said hesitantly, her mask that blended in with her ghillie suit muffled her voice.

"I found some bandages in your bag and patched myself up a bit," he said. "I hope that's okay."

"No worries on that."

"Can I see your face?" Christian asked.

With a deep breath, Shadow pulled the mask up to reveal who she truly was, and Christian laughed in surprise.

"Shana, from when we picked up food," Christian grinned. "It seems fate wasn't done with us yet."

"I don't know, you said that you were okay never seeing her again when you thought I was someone else." She moved to her gear that she had already packed up to load in her truck.

"And fate just proved that you're one and the same and I'm a very lucky man," he answered. Christian turned her to him slowly. "The next thing I need to ask is, baby, be mine?"

"Isn't that kinda in poor taste?"

"Not when it's being said by a psychopathic cartel leader and murderer."

"Cheesy, then?" Shana countered.

He tweaked her nose. "I can deal with it if you can."

Impulsively she pulled his head down for a quick kiss but instead her lips lingered.

She cleared her throat. "Well, how do you feel about checking out South Carolina?"

"I could be persuaded," Christian drawled. "But how do I get my stuff from a destroyed, shot-up apartment that is going to be crawling with the police and probably the feds?"

"With finesse," Shana said. "Grab some of these packs. I'll show you where a sniper who misses a bed and actual sleep stays until she can leave for home."

"Some strange, dingy, nondescript hotel in Jersey?" Christian asked.

Shana snorted. "Bite your tongue. I go five-star, baby."

"I think I might like this riding-off-into-the-sunset thing," he teased.

"Stick with me, kid, and I'll show you the world."

He opened the door so Shana could step through in front of him and, as she passed by, he pressed a soft kiss at her temple. It was becoming clearer by the moment, the wall she placed around her life wasn't always necessary, and a sniper's life didn't mean she has to be alone. *One year left and that won't matter*, she thought. It was time for her to see life beyond the scope of a rifle.

JENNIFER GRAESER DORNBUSH

THE GIRL IS MINE

Paisley Vivian Nelson

Belnap is crusty. And I'm getting crusty.

Seventeen is too young to be crusty. If I don't get outta here soon, I'll be dried up by the time I'm eighteen.

The only time I ever have any fun here in Belnap, population 3,921, is when the gin runners come up from Chicago.

They stay at the Courtright, not only because it's the only decent lodging in town. But because it runs along the river that snakes across the western part of the state, then meets up with Lake Michigan at the town of Spring Harbor. From here, the shipping boats leave thrice a day for Chicago.

I'm not supposed to know this, but underneath the Courtright is a large hidden barrel house in the cellar and a tunnel system that leads down to the river so the gin runner won't get caught.

The gin runners are good-hearted men all-in-all and I don't mind having them in Belnap. I'm not afraid of them. I don't know anyone who is. They don't cause trouble. The police turn a blind eye. And they keep our store owners flush with green.

And they always stay at the Courtright. They have money. Not honest money. Money from running booze barrels down the river to Chicago. But it spends just fine.

The Courtright is the only place in Belnap that has what I would call charm. The suites overlook the river. Their walls are draped in velvet paper and velvet curtains and velvet bedspreads. There's a dining room on the main floor with a band and dancing on Friday and Saturday nights.

Five course dinners. Waiters wear tuxes. Hostesses—that's me— wear evening gowns. I can only afford two that I alternate between on Friday and Saturday nights. I'm not allowed to work on Sundays. Have to be at church. Morning and evening worship. And Sunday school in between.

The Courtright is so fancy that we even have private room service. The food kind. And also, the lady kind. I'm not supposed to know that either. And I'm not supposed to know who provides the services, but I do know one of the gals. Priscilla Garmond graduated three years my senior. I'm also not supposed to know that she got pregnant by one of them. Which was why she disappeared for five months to go visiting her aunt in Indiana.

When she came back to the Courtright, she fell in love with another one of them. Before you could blink a false eyelash, she was off with him to Chicago. Lucky girl.

I wish I could move to Chicago. They're having fun in Chicago.

I used to have fun. With Wesley. That feels like a long time ago. But there was a war and three years in between then and now. I was a freshman and Wesley was a senior. We dated that entire school year till he went off to Europe with the army. When he left, he made me promise to marry him. I was fourteen, almost fifteen. How could I know what love was? We had fun. Was that all love was supposed to be?

Wes came back a couple months ago. Different. Mature. Serious. And crusty.

Wes doesn't like that I work the Courtright with all those

THE GIRL IS MINE

loose men running around. I told him, "I have my daddy's blessing. Why not yours?" To which he turned all growly and balled his fists. To which I turned around and walked away. To which he yanked me back by the shoulder and nearly pulled my arm out of its socket.

"Stop it. You want me to tell Pa you're hitting me?"

"Sorry, I don't mean to—these things in me get all gnarled up sometimes."

"Things?"

"Memories . . . what I saw over there."

"Maybe it would help if you talked about it?"

"Doing what married people do in bed will help."

"Why would I wanna marry a crusty old man like you?"

"The war turned my hair gray."

"Why do we gotta rush it? I'm still in high school."

"You need to grow up, Paisley. I can't wait forever."

"Then, let's not."

But I wasn't ready to marry him. So, to get him off my back, we head to an abandoned warehouse near his father's steel foundry.

That was fun.

And it bided me some time. But the Courtright was my escape. My excuse for not having to spend all my free time with Wes.

One evening, after the dinner rush, I got called to take a tray to room 214. Mr. Marion Hollister. There was no funny business. I promise you that. He knows my father is the Methodist minister because Pa takes up residence down by the river where Mr. Hollister and his crew load out their casks of hooch.

Pa does what he can to get them to mend their heathen ways. Pa's no snitch and the gin runners like to keep him around. He's a good conversationalist. But when they need Pa to scram, they send him on some charity errand. Pa falls for it every time. Poor, crusty chap doing what he can to save the lost. *Pearls to swine*, I told him. *You're just throwing pearls to swine.*

Hollister and his men are just not law-abiding citizens.

"Especially when the law is so dumb," said Hollister.

"I don't know much about laws. But I do know people. And people gotta drink and smoke."

"You're a smart gal."

"Thank you, Mr. Hollister."

"Nah—call me Viper."

I laugh. And then I feel badly. I've hurt his feelings; he doesn't show it.

"Guess that does sound kinda silly to a girl from Belnap."

"I should get back to the floor."

"Yeah. I know . . . you're not that type of girl."

I hand Marion his tray and he takes the plate of food and sees me to the door with a generous ten dollar tip. I thank him and pocket the tip, thinking that it will cover new material for a third evening gown.

"I've heard you singing."

"You have? At church?"

"I ain't been to no church. Around the dining hall. After the dining hall closes and you're doing set ups for the breakfast service. You have a beautiful, beautiful voice. I could listen forever."

"You ever been to any church?"

"No. But I'm human. I have a soul too."

"I'm not judging. I leave that job to my father. I should go."

"I mean it, Viv."

"Viv? My name's Paisley."

"Your middle name's Vivian, ain't it?"

"How'd you know?"

"Paisley Vivian Nelson! I heard your pa yell it when he wanted you to come up from the river. Boy, did you jump when he called out."

The Viper laughs now. His face is honest. Yearning. Soft, even. Just around the eyes. I don't take offense. I'm surprised he was paying attention to me at all.

"I'm not kidding you, doll. Voice like a goddess."

"No one's ever told me that before."

"You ever think about heading outta Belnap?"

"To where?"

"You could rival the best club singers in Chi-town."

Viv. I kinda like the sound of that. It's grown up. Sultry.
Not a bit crusty.

———

Wesley Milton

I returned from France, June 2, 1919, and went directly to Paisley's
house to ask for her hand. I was told by the Reverend Percival Nelson
that I had to wait until Paisley graduated from high school the following June before I married her. I had already waited three years. What
was one more, the Reverend told me.

I waited three months.

Saturday night of Labor Day weekend I presented the ring to Paisley and slid it on her finger.

I didn't see any twinkle in her eyes. Not even a smile. She kept staring at that ring like it was a spider she wanted to swat off her hand.

"Don't you wanna show your ma?"

"It's late. She'll probably be asleep."

"She'll be up waiting to see you."

"I want to take a walk. Down by the river. Alone."

"There's nothing but drunks and gin runners down by the river now
that the sun's set. It's not safe."

"Have you told your folks?"

"My mom helped me pick out the ring."

"Tell her it's very nice."

"Very nice? Is that all you can say?"

"It is. What do you want me to say?"

"I spend three years walking in French mud, slinging artillery, and
all you can offer up is 'nice'?"

"I don't mean to sound ungrateful, Wes. I'm just in shock. That's all."

I coulda slept with silk-faced girls like Paisley in every little French countryside town. But I didn't. I only slipped up twice. And each time was after a couple shell-shocked weeks on the battlefield. Paisley could never understand. The intensity. The horror. The bloody dreams.

The need for release. I'll never mention it to her. She'll never need to know. It'll drift out of my brain once we're married, and the babies come. And life turns to addictive monotony at my father's steel mill.

Nice?

Waiting for her wasn't nice. It was hell.

I follow Paisley down to the river, approaching the gin runners who are loading up their flatboat. Paisley twists her engagement ring around to hide the diamond in her palm. Then, she slips her hand into her dress pockets. They talk for a long time until my blood's hot as an active battlefield and I know if I go down there, someone will end up dead.

Paisley waits on the sidelines until I see that gin runner motion to her and pull her aside. There's that twinkle in her eye that I've been longing for.

The next morning I've calmed enough to go to her house to confront her about it. Her mother calls up to her room. Paisley never sleeps in this late. But they made an exception last night, Mrs. Nelson tells me, because Paisley was with me, and she knows we have a lot to talk about now that there's a wedding to plan.

Have we set a date yet, she wonders, because Paisley didn't have a lot to say about it at 2:00 a.m., coming home smelling like liquor and cigarettes. She and the Reverend don't approve of the pub, just to be clear. But this time, it's an exception. There have to be exceptions in life, she believes. She hopes they will be getting married soon. It's not good to let one's passions get the best of us.

One of Paisley's little brothers calls down to us. Her clothes—including her two gowns—are missing. Her toiletries, pillow, and a few personal items are also missing. And she left this.

Little brother ran to me and stuck his hand out. Pinched between his thumb and forefinger was Paisley's engagement ring.

———

Marion Hollister
(a.k.a. Viper)

I picked her up at Union Station. She came on my dime, and I took her directly to the north shore apartment where I had set her up with Jossie, another hostess at Clive's Club.

When I opened the door to the fifth floor, single-room apartment, Paisley dropped her bag and went right for the window. Outside was an unobstructed portrait of Lake Michigan. She beamed at the view like she had just discovered there actually was gold at the end of a rainbow.

"What'd your folks say when you left?"

"Nothing."

"You didn't tell 'em, did ya? You leave a note?"

"'Course not. I don't want them to come looking."

"They will, anyhow."

"No. They're Swedish and stubborn."

"I know the type."

"Where're your folks?"

"Virginia. Last I saw them."

"They dead?"

"Maybe. It's been years."

"What about that fiancé?"

"I didn't know you knew."

"I saw the ring. What'd you do with it?"

"Don't need it."

"He gonna come here causing trouble?"

She peeled herself from the window with a look that told me she had never considered that part before.

"It's hard to say."

"No worries, doll. We'll handle it."

"How?"

"How we do."

"I know things about what you do . . . how it's done."

"Well, try to forget. Okay?"

"I don't judge. I leave that to my father."

She turned back to the window. Viper found it amusing how she plastered her face and hands to the glass. As if she were looking at a dream.

"You can go to the lake anytime you want, Viv. It's just a short walk."

"Viv? You like that name, huh?"

"You've got a chance to be whoever you wanna be here."

"Vivian sounds nicer than Viv. But I'm tired of being nice."

"Who do you wanna be, Viv?"

"I wanna be someone great."

"All right then. We've got some work to do."

I told her to trash those old gowns and I took her to Macy's for new ones. Clive's Club was elite and elegant. She needed to look the part. Viv opened up to all of it. High heels. Plunging necklines. Slits up the sides. Red rouge and red lips. When it was all finished, I had created what was probably my best gal to date.

Viv was a good hostess, but that wasn't her selling point. She was gonna make money for us with song. After a month I convinced Clive we should get her on stage. We had a little help from a horn player who seemed to latch himself to the girl. I made it clear to him he needed to keep his distance. For one, he was Black. And as progressive as things was getting in the Windy City, it just weren't fitting. Clive didn't need no trouble and neither did I. They started rehearsals immediately early mornings and late nights after hours.

On stage, in three-inch stilettos Viv was unstoppable. Wasn't a melody she couldn't master after hearing it only one time.

"Where'd ya learn to sing like that?"

"What do you think?"

"Probably the only good thing to ever come outta church."

"I don't miss church. I never felt God there. When I sing, on that stage, it's like I feel like God's right next to me."

"Maybe He is."

"I don't think He'd approve of the way I look."

"God made you gorgeous. What's wrong with that?"

Her face flushed underneath those rouge cheeks.

"Pa'd probably say that's blasphemous."

"You miss him?"

"I miss my ma. My brothers."

"You should write her. Mothers worry."

"Did yours?"

"Not mine, doll."

"What was wrong with her?"

"Almost everything. You should write your mother."

"Ma'll see the postmark's from Chicago."

"I'll drop it secretly to her next time I'm in Belnap."

"You would do that for me?"

Of course. Anything.

But I didn't say it.

I had done good getting Viv for the club. And Clive knew it. Once he saw how attractive she was . . . how she lit up a room . . . how his club went from crusty to waitlist desirable overnight. Well, Clive wiped out my debt entirely.

This was a true miracle seeing as my debt to Clive was to the tune of two hundred barrels of moonshine. I had misjudged the weather and a freak Lake Michigan storm took the whole shipment as I was transporting them from Spring Harbor to Chicago. I had been in deep to Clive, the club, and those who owned both . . . Capone's network. And now I was free.

Thanks to Viv.

Once my debt was cleared, Clive owned Viv. And I no longer had a say in her fate. Normally, I don't give a rat's hairy ass. But I was protective of Paisley.

Clive was greedy and Clive saw humans as commodities. He would stretch her to the limits, squeezing every dollar out of her.

———

Julius Rockafeller

When I met Paisley that fall at the club, she was busting her way through a long list of nevers.

Never missed a Sunday in church.

Never wrote back to her family.

Never heard a lick of the jazz beat.

Never been in a mixed-race club.

Never stayed out all night.

Never been kissed by a Black person.

Never been to jail.

With cash from Clive, we bailed her and a host of servers and band members, out of what had been a routine club raid.

When we stepped out of the city jail onto the city streets just after 1:00 a.m., Paisley looped her arm into mine and looked up at me, brown eyes full of the city.

"Well, that wasn't so bad after all. Are you hungry? I'm hungry."

I took her to a café to drink coffee and eat buttered toast and jam. She talked the entire time, even entertaining a few other middle-of-the-night patrons. When the owner kicked us out at four, Paisley wanted more.

"What do we do now?"

"We sleep."

"I'm not tired."

"We can walk."

"I could walk forever."

So we walked. Miles. All the way north on the lake shore to where the path ended, and the rocks took over the shoreline.

I never had a chance to return home with my trumpet, so I sat down on the edge of the seawall and started to play. The sun rose to the tune of "Cuban Moon." Paisley was feeling frisky and frivolous. She danced and made up her own lyrics while I riffed. They was pretty dang good lyrics. And confirmed what I had believed all along. She was so much more than just a singer.

She was an original.

I'm sure no one close to her had ever told her that before. You don't tell that to someone and then expect them to stick around town. Her ma and pa must have been wise to that secret, too, because Paisley kept her dreams tidy and managed.

When I finally pulled my horn from my tired lips and set it aside, Paisley slumped down next to me, disappointed. She lay her head on my shoulder and was quiet. We sat on the seawall, her thigh touching mine; spray-off from the lake's waves soaked our legs.

The club was enough for someone like me to aspire to. But Paisley . . . the world needed to know her. You don't hide a gift like that under a bushel. So, I told her.

"We could start an act."

"What do you mean?"

"You singin'. Me playin'."

"And do what then?"

"Head to New York."

"The city that never sleeps."

"Would suit you then."

"Just you and me?"

"Why not?"

"Singin' and playin'. For whom?"

"Whoever wants to hire us."

"Where would we live?"

"We'll make friends."

"How would we live?"

"What do you mean?"

"Would we marry?"

I shrugged. And she didn't like that.

"Do you want to marry?"

Now she shrugged. And I didn't take offense.

"I want to sing. I feel good when I'm singing. And I want to be with you. I feel good with I'm with you."

"Then it's decided."

"When do we go?"

"Once we work up an act and we're ready."

"I see. What'll that take?"

"What's your arrangement?"

"I don't understand."

"With Mr. Clive. How long did he sign you on to work?"

"I never signed anything."

"Did you sign something?"

I shook my head.

"I don't mean literally signed a paper. A handshake agreement. That's what we have."

"I don't have that. Is that bad?"

"How long did you agree to work for him?"

"It was never discussed."

"Mr. Clive'll be upset to see you go."

"Should I be worried about it?"

"No, sweetie. You gotta live your life. Right?"

"Let's get our plan together first. Then, I'll talk to him."

"We'll talk to him."

The sun was now sitting atop the lake-water horizon, its morning rays bounced off my horn at just the right angle to blind me. Wincing made me sleepy. My bones was creaky and I wanted my bed with Paisley next to me.

"Let's go home."

"Not yet. I'm hungry."

"Again?"

"Adrenaline's got me all juiced up."

"Adrenaline? For what?"

"The future. How long do you think it'll take to be ready?"

"I dunno. Couple months."

"That'll give us time to save up."

"We can rehearse at your apartment. Not the club. Will Jossie mind?"

"Doubt it. She spends a good deal of time at Rico's."

"Come on, doll. Let's get an omelet and head to bed."

———

Midmorning at the club next day, I'm alone in the music pit, hammering through a few new riffs when I sense someone towering over me from the stage.

"Have you slept with her yet?"

It's Clive.

I set my horn in my lap and look up.

"Ain't none of your business."

"You're both my business."

"Not outside these four walls."

"That's not up for debate."

"What do you want from her?"

"Delilah's leaving. Getting married."

"A client?"

Clive nodded.

"And you allowed that?"

"For a price."

Everything was for a price at the club.

"Why Paisley? Pick someone else."

"She's in demand. People are asking."

"She's your lead. You're gonna lose your lead."

"I'll find a new lead."

"You don't just find talent like that."

"I can charge more because she's the lead."

"She ain't cut out for it."

"She'll only get the best clients."

"I don't like this."

"You've done it before. What's the matter?"

"I did it once. Once only. No more."

I went very still, keep my eyes on my horn, my fingers silently working the keys through a melody in my head.

"You gotta do it, you understand? Cause if ya ain't . . . well, horn players a dime dozen now, coming up from the south. No one's gonna miss you. And I know you've got no kin to scrap you up. Do we have an understanding?"

I look beyond Clive to the empty tables in the auditorium and Paisley, fresh and clean in a new dress, strutting toward me.

"I know you like her. You can still have her. I'm not stopping you from that."

It doesn't work that way. Once you break 'em . . . they're broken.

"Julius, do we have an understanding?"

"It takes time. I need time."

"You have a month."

He tossed a thin stack of ten spots, and they fluttered down around me.

As he turned to go there was Paisley smiling at both of us as she approached.

"Good day, Mr. Clive."

"Vivian. How are you, sweetheart? You look lovely. Got a full house again tonight."

———

Dilbert Clive III

"Mr. Clive. Say, do you have a moment?"

She was a sweet thing. A curious one. Voice like an angel. Not afraid to speak her smart mind. This was her biggest fault. Viper had a thing for the saucy ones. And this one was getting too big for her britches.

"Anything for you, sweetheart."

"Is there an arrangement between us?"

"What do you mean, honey?"

"A contract? Between you and me."

"We don't need that. You and I can talk about anything. Am I right?"

"Yes. And in that case, I think I deserve a raise."

"You do? Why's that now?"

"I've been your lead for almost four months now. Crowds are growing. Lines out the door. I see what kinda tips the other girls are pulling in slinging drinks."

"You're a star. What more do you want?"

"I want a cut."

"Don't you enjoy your job here?"

"Except for the raids."

"You always get bailed out."

She laughed. I laughed too. It was good to build confidence.

"You're gonna get raided at any club in town."

"True. But I might also get more money."

"You so sure about that?"

"I've had offers."

"Have you?"

Was it a bluff? I had lost Caitlyn last summer to the Regency at the Miracle Mile on account of a scout.

"Let's give it another couple months. If sales are still up, we'll talk about a raise."

"Could be too late by then. Ma says church donations are down. Pa's depressed about it. Says attendance is down too. I'd like to help out."

I hated the church almost as much as I hated being lied to.

I took Viv by the arm, a fatherly gesture. Nothing in my composure to alarm her.

"You're a charitable young lady. That's part of your charm. I'll see what I can do."

"Thank you, Mr. Clive. Hilda's waiting for me in the dressing room."

I gave her a couple bills.

"Buy yourself a new gown. You're a star. Stay bright, sweetheart."

I sent her off with a little swat on the rear.

Viv gave me a wink and flitted away, counting her cash.

With every great talent, there is always . . . eventually . . . those damned demands. And now that there are demands, I cannot risk Julius's gentle grooming.

I headed toward the bar, I could feel the eyes on my back. Julius watching.

His horn let out a piercing wail as I left. His way of slapping me.

Viv's a good girl. As good as they come. Damned preacher's daughters. Why was it, seemed they were always the worst? She had tasted the good life and allowed that seed of greed to sprout. And if I let it, it will grow into a thick, thick stalk. It'll choke out everything I've built.

Shame.

There was only one thing to do. Nip it in the bud.

———

Julius Rockafeller

A little more than a week went by. I couldn't bring myself to sell her out yet. I was too busy planning our escape.

During Friday night's performance, I caught up with Paisley during intermission. She was feeling lightheaded and nauseous. She dove for the bathroom.

When the curtain went up twenty minutes later and it was Jossie who showed up on stage, I knew Clive had played me.

I was out the backstage door as soon as my last note cut off.

I found Paisley's apartment door wide open, and Paisley curled up on the couch. Stone-faced. Mascara smeared down her white cheeks. She was in her robe. And she was shaking and singing ever so softly her lyrics to "Cuban Moon."

From the bathroom sink I heard the trickle of water overflowing and saw the flooded floor. I dashed in to turn the faucet off. A pair of bloody panties was clogging the sink drain. Next to the clawfoot tub was her new lavender gown. The collar was ripped, a sleeve was missing, and the hem of the dress was wet and muddy.

I rushed back to Paisley and knelt by her side. Didn't know whether to touch her or not. Her eyes didn't seem to register that I was there.

"Baby? Babydoll. It's me. Julius. Can you hear me?"

Her eyes blinked once but did not find me. I used my index finger to stroke her hand. She flinched and tucked it under her chest.

"I saw you talking to him."

"Who?"

"Clive."

"Clive talks to me."

"Whatever he said made you angry."

"It was business."

"Did you tell him we wanted to leave?"

"No. He's trying to cheat us musicians."

"No. He sent a guy to do this."

"I didn't say a word. It was our secret, Babydoll. I swear."

"Did you know?"

"Of course not."

"You betrayed me."

"Clive betrayed me!"

"What do you mean?"

"It was gonna happen sooner or later. That bastard wanted me to get you to service some of the club guests."

"And you were gonna do it?"

"I was gonna get us outta here."

"That man who . . . he told me . . . he'd kill me and my family if I ever left Clive. What's he talking about, Julius? What have I gotten myself into?"

"We'll get out of this. I promise."

"You're in it too, then?"

"They don't own us."

Tears poured from Paisley's eyes now, but she still didn't move a muscle of her body or so much as lift her head up.

"Tell me . . . who did this to you? I'll make this right."

"You're no killer."

"Baby, please."

"It was dark."

"Did you even get a tiny glimpse?"

"He put a . . . put my dress over my face."

"Baby—"

"He smelled fishy."

"Someone from the docks. Let's go to the police."

"With what cards in our favor?" She laughed from her dry throat, which sent her into a coughing fit. Soon, Paisley was hacking up bloody saliva and wiping it away with the sleeve of her robe.

"God. Paisley. He hit you!?"

"I can't feel it. Can't feel anything."

"You should go to the hospital."

She shook her head.

I left her side only long enough to rummage through the sparse kitchen cupboards until I found a small bottle of bootlegged whiskey.

"Just a few sips, Babydoll."

She wet her lips on the rim and I was able to get a few sips down her throat.

Paisley slumped back into the couch, curling her feet into the cushions. She became very still but she still wouldn't let me hold her hand.

After a few moments, her eyes became a bit brighter. The taut look on her face relaxed. I gave her a few more sips. I slipped a bolster pillow under her head to support it.

"Don't move. I'll make some tea."

"Is Jossie coming home tonight?"

"No. She's been staying at Rico's."

"I'll stay with you."

"No."

"You can't stay alone."

"I don't want you here. I don't want to see you."

"Don't be like that. I didn't know—"

"Go. And leave the door like you found it."

"You crazy? He could come back—"

"I don't care if I die."

"I do."

"If he wanted to kill me he would have done it already."

"You're not well. I'm staying."

"Get out, Julius."

She took the mug of whiskey and hurled it at me with such great force that when it shattered, pieces of it sliced clear through my thick matted hair into my scalp.

"I love you, Paisley. Please—I'm sorry."

"Get on now! I got other problems to worry about."

———

The Reverend
Alton Percival Nelson
(a.k.a. Percy)

They called it wander-*lust* for a reason. Lust was always at the center of any grave sin.

Percy didn't know where Paisley's wanderlust came from.

Maybe being pent up in a small town.

Maybe seeing Wesley and the others go off to war.

Maybe all those magazines she purchased from the Five & Dime.

Maybe it was being around all those bootleggers at the inn.

Percy had prided himself in not giving into the temptation to chase after her when Paisley left. The Prodigal Daughter would sow her wild oats and return to them when she was hungry . . . hungry for forgiveness. And he the earthy father, along with her heavenly Father would grant her pardon, kill the fatted calf, and host a church potluck in her honor.

They got the only letter Paisley had ever written to the family three days ago. It was addressed to Ma. She was doing well. A headline singer at a fancy club on Clark Street. She made a salary. She loved Chicago. And she was saving her money because soon there would be two of them to support. She was pregnant. She didn't want any questions and didn't need their help. She just wanted them to know and to send her love.

Percy's precious sacrifice to God the Father was tarnished goods.

Percy exited his train at Union Station to face this Sodom of a city and find his lost sheep. It was harder than imagined. He had not expected Chicago to be thundering with machinery. He had not expected to see so many buildings. He had not expected to be accosted by stinking, mangled vagrants. He had not expected the street workers to be so desperate. The stockyards so bloody. The wealthy so disoriented. There was so much saving to be done. Suddenly felt a longing for the mediocrity of Belnap.

Percy saw something in Paisley from the first time she sang "Jesus Loves Me" at age two. But he channeled it immediately into something holy and honorable. Paisley was consecrated to the Lord. He did this because of her mother. Paisley was born middle of seven. Three older brothers. Three younger ones. Ma said that once boys become men, they move on quickly. Once they get wives, the wives take over and turn to their own mothers. Daughters stay close to mothers like that. And daughters should stay close to home. There were grandbabies to consider, remember. Ma wanted Paisley placed neatly in the same box she had been placed years before by her own mother. There were some traditions you held onto.

Percy knew Paisley's gift had great worth in the wider world. It would only be a matter of time before someone from that wider world would bounce into town and see what Percy saw. And Paisley was not to leave Belnap. This was her mother's unspoken wish. And it must be respected because Ma didn't ever ask for anything but this. She took, quite literally, the verse in Corinthians about submissive wives; and this became a point of pride for Percy.

Percy felt that no one really understood Paisley like he did. Therefore, Paisley's specialness had to be used for the church. To keep her close to Belnap, he kept her close to the church. Training her up in the way of the Lord and honing Paisley's talent for God. Paisley spent hours memorizing the hymns. More hours in piano lessons. And, once her feet reached the pedals of the organ, still more hours under the instruction of the church organist. She sang in the church choir. She sang for weddings. She sang for funerals. She sang for the Christmas and Easter services. Her gift was from God and the Reverend Percival Nelson saw to it that she gave it back to her Creator. Whether in the form of praise or penance.

But he was sure of one thing, Paisley could not sing her way out of this predicament.

Going door to door, Percy found Clive's Club on Clark Street. He snuck into the shadows and watched. His daughter's performance left him shaking at his core. Her voice had deepened into a seductive womanliness, the kind that moved men to lustful desires. Oh, Christ have mercy!

His anger was a righteous one, a roaring white-hot furnace, like the one that was meant to incinerate Shadrach, Meshach, and Abednego. He kept hidden until Paisley exited the stage for the night. Then, he went backstage, found her in her dressing room, and with superhuman force, removed his daughter from her den of iniquity.

———

Wesley Milton

Mrs. Nelson paid me a visit at my father's foundry when I was coming off shift to tell me that Paisley was pregnant. She thought perhaps it was mine and would I see to Paisley in Chicago. They would welcome her home. They would welcome both of us to the marriage altar. Would I try? Please. For the sake of her grandchild?

I hid myself by the back door of the club where I knew the employees came and went. I'm going to get Paisley back. Or at least get her to listen to me.

Through the evening hours, many came and went. But none with Paisley's height. Paisley's build. Paisley's voice. Or Paisley's confident swagger.

After 1:00 a.m., a single woman emerged, coat buttoned to the neck. Face and hair shrouded in a head wrap, wool gloves protecting from the biting wind that sliced through the buildings. She had Paisley's height. Paisley's build. Paisley's confident swagger.

What do I say to her? Even her name escaped my lips.

Paisley lit a cigarette without missing a single beat in her step. I knew she had tried her brother's back in Belnap. Now it was a habit.

I began to trail her and licked my lips.

"Paisley? Pais—?"

She didn't turn. Not even a brief glance over the shoulder.

Maybe she didn't hear me.

Paisley took a shortcut through the alley. She moved with purpose, clipping along, avoiding the potholes and little piles of garbage. I followed with kitten steps. It was dark all through the city. Even darker between the buildings, where the alleys were void of streetlamps.

"Pais— I didn't drive all the way down here to chase you!"

She picked up the pace, heels clipping on the pavement. I ran after her, flaming with rage that she wouldn't even talk to me. Not even a glance. I sprinted forward; knife pointed out at the hip. I was on her heels.

"Paisley Vivian Nelson! You stop right now! If you don't . . . I'll shoot!"

She stopped so abruptly that I ran the knife into her lower back, all eight inches, slicing into that space between the pelvic bones to the nest where life first ignites.

My grip was still tight on the knife as she gasped for breath.

She stumbled forward a few steps and dropped to her knees. The knife was still in my hands and blood was pooling under her knees. Not a word was voiced; but a gurgling and a straining to breathe.

"I love you, Paisley. I would have treated you good!"

Her head nodded, up and down . . . gripping her belly she slumped to the ground.

I knelt to her side and grabbed at her shoulder, shaking her.

"Can't you understand? None of this had to happen if you—"

But the life was already out of her.

"Pais— I didn't mean to. I don't know what— Paisley. I love you, sweetheart."

I screamed. Then, capped my own palm over my mouth. What a sissy was I? I shamed myself silently and turned her over to examine my deed. Her scarf and hair fell across her face. It was a good thing, too, because I couldn't bear to look on her face and I couldn't bare those eyes to look on me. I saw that the knife had come clean through to the other side. I hoped I had sliced through that baby as well.

Damn her. And damn those brown eyes that never sparkled for me. That sparkled for some other man . . . a drifter . . . a crook! I murdered and mutilated for my flag. Why couldn't she see I was the better man?

I plunged my knife into her eyes and carved them out from her sockets.

When a light flickered on from a nearby apartment building, I came to my senses. This was no battlefield, and I was a soldier. I wasn't about to get caught, arrested, and imprisoned—all for doing what soldiers are trained to do.

Moving quickly, I rolled the horrible whore toward the river, waded in with the body until I was waist deep. I shoved her underwater and held her there. I might have held on forever had I not heard a stir from across the river which jolted me again to my senses. I released my grip. The current began to turn the body face up. And as her corpse swept past me, hair splayed out behind her head, I saw that it was not the face of my Paisley. But of a stranger.

I slapped my face with the dank river water and emerged under the cover of night up, disappearing into the city.

I laid tracks back to Belnap, arriving just before daylight and coasting the car into my father's foundry. The third shifters were slinking away from the factory to disappear into the street . . . some to their houses . . . some to the pubs . . . some to the river where the bootleggers lay in wait to pawn off their jugs of third-rate batch for nickels and dimes.

I made my way to one of the molten steel vats. And took my knife from my pocket.

When it had been swallowed up by the liquid metal, I rolled a hundred-pound steel coil down to the river. I attached a rope around it, then secured the other end around my waist . . . and dragged it in with me until my feet no longer touched the riverbed.

———

Dr. Forrest Jessup
Office of Coroner
City of Chicago

It wasn't the first time I'd seen this man before in his morgue. If he had to guess, he was most likely tied to Capone's men, probably a lower-level minion. Although this stiff was not one of Capone's jobs. For a change.

"Her body was discovered floating up the Chicago River, by a couple of stockyard workers. Based on the stage of decomposition of the corpse, she was killed between last Thursday and Monday. One stab wound clean through the torso. She would have been conscious for a few minutes until she finally passed out from the loss of blood."

I don't mean to be so casual, but I'm getting a little hardened to this kind of event. Unfortunately, these girls are a dime a dozen. Lots of them coming to the big city from Iowa, Ohio, Indiana, Michigan, Pennsylvania. Even as far as the East Coast. They come here single. Alone. Vulnerable. No plan other than to "find a job." What does that mean? How does that look? Most haven't a clue. They've never had to do that before. Trouble soon seeks them out. And before they know it, they're in the wrong place with the wrong people. I'm sure they were good girls back home. But you get desperate here. You get tempted. You think you're invincible. And you're hungry.

The cut isn't clean. The flesh is jagged and torn. An in and out job. My guess, an eight- or nine-inch serrated blade. Would have been painful going in. Worse coming out. This girl suffered. No doubt about that.

"So? She one of yours?"

"Yeah, the girl is mine."

"What's her name?"

"What's it matter."

"For my report."

"Forget your report. No one cares."

"Her family might. What do you want me to do with her?"

"I don't want her."

"Send for the family."

"They're not on speaking terms."

"Then we bury her in the city cemetery. That's where all the John and Jane Does go."

"But she's not a Jane Doe."

"She is if you're not gonna take her."

"Who hated her so much?"

"Why does it have to be hate?"

"She deserves a proper burial."

"With what money?"

"Your boss has money. I know that. And his boss has money."

"What do you know?"

"I know that it's getting old cleaning up your messes."

"She ain't my mess."

"She ain't mine either."

"How much to leave her?"

"A thousand."

"You crook."

"She's already been stinking up my shop for days."

"Five hundred."

"This isn't a negotiation."

"Everything is for sale."

"Not me. So, what'll it be?"

"I'll call Calumet & Sons. Have her out of here by end of day."

———

Viv

I have big lungs. Huge inflatable singer lungs.

And after Pa gave me a good and proper shove into the river, I used those lungs to capture and hold all my breath as I dove deep down underwater, fighting my way to the Y.

Here, the Chicago River diverges, one branch feeding from the north, and one from the south. I took the northbound branch, swimming until I was sure I would be out of Pa's sight. But then, just in case, when I finally surfaced for air, I kept my face flush with the water line, floating on my back, body sunk below the surface, until I got far, far up past the bend to Goose Island. Here I stroked my way to shore, drug myself out, and zigzagged my way through the city back to my apartment.

Viper was there waiting for me with a long face and bottle of whiskey half gone. He jumped up when he saw me and threw his arms around me. Eventually, he peeled himself from me and touched my draggled, damp hair.

"Where's the preacher?"

"Don't worry about him. He's not coming round again."

"Baby, what happened?"

"Not now."

I went to the bedroom and exchanged my wet clothes for a bathrobe. Viper followed, wanting an answer.

"I'm starving."

"I gotta tell you something. I got called down to the morgue. Jossie . . ."

"No . . . please . . . how did she . . . ?"

"Murdered. Someone stabbed her good and plenty. Even took her eyes out."

The news dropped me to the floor. Viper moved me to the sofa. Pours me glass.

"Who did this? Was she in trouble with Clive?"

"No. I dunno. Who knows?"

The whiskey went down quick.

"Last I knew, she was staying at Rico's place. They were a thing. Did he tell you?"

Viper nodded.

"She's spent a lot of time with Rico—"

"It wasn't Rico. He was out on a job with me."

"Cops gonna do anything?"

"Not reporting it. Paid off the coroner."

The cops wouldn't have lifted a finger for someone like Jossie anyhow.

"I'll write to her family."

Their address was most likely on the unopened letters she stashed in a shoe box in the corner of the closet. I should send those back. Or maybe not. Why rub salt in a wound?

"I gotta ask you something, Viv."

I handed him my empty glass and he poured another.

"You shouldn't be drinking in your condition."

"How you know about that?"

"I don't mind. I've always wanted a family."

"It's not yours."

"I know."

"Will you care for this child?"

"Of course. Like it's my own."

"Even though he won't look like you."

"He's part of you. Do you love Julius?"

"Is that what you wanted to ask me?"

"No. But I need to know."

"Julius betrayed me."

"He's gonna be heated you ran off with his baby."

"No child of mine is going to know a rat like that for a father."

"I asked if you love him?"

"I love what he gave me."

"It's gonna be hard. I mean, the color."

"So what? We're all a bunch of mutts here."

"Who told you that?"

"My ma used to say it. You know the funny thing about mutts?"

"What's that?"

"They love you just as much as the purebreds."

The Viper laughed at that. I think I might be the only one in the world who gets to hear him laugh. Then, he came to my side and kissed me. It was the most tender kiss I've ever felt.

"I love you, Viv."

I searched those green eyes planted on mine.

"Did you hear me? I love you, Viv."

"Yeah. I heard you."

I thought about how beautiful it would be for my baby to have an emerald-eyed sibling someday.

And I thought about how Pa had me dangled over the bridge, spewing out his vengeance. And how joy flushed through me as his vice grip released. Sweet freedom! I disappeared under the murky river waters, diving deep; carried away with the upstream current.

I knew, now, his real saving could begin.

"I love you, too, Marion."

I grabbed my suitcase and gathered my dresses. Then, I went into

Jossie's closet for the shoebox and her gowns.

"Whadda ya doin', Babydoll?"

"Let's go West," I said. "Chicago's gettin' crusty."

HEATHER GRAHAM

THRILLER

"Don't you look at me like that!" Riley Jordan told Rocket, Ethan Warner's rottweiler.

The dog wouldn't hurt her—she was pretty sure. He seemed to understand that she was coming daily to let him—and Ethan's other three dogs—out to run around for a while, have their food bowls filled, and last, but hardly least, pick up the poop in the house that they couldn't hold in until she arrived.

She wasn't sure that a dog could shrug, but if so, Rocket shrugged and went off to run in the yard, then turned back to look at her.

"Hey, a dog is supposed to be man's best friend!" she said, shaking her head as the dog continued to study her. Judging her, sizing her up.

"Man, you know, as in humankind, man, woman. And you know what? There are people who think that dogs are just best all around, better than people."

The dog kept staring.

Did dogs think? Was he weighing her up? Did they know right from wrong? Sure, at the very least—they learned they were *supposed* to do their business outside.

Penny, Percy, and Petunia, the three small fluffy mutt pups who completed her friend's dog family, liked to woof, and run around her, longing for pets and attention—as well as treats. They'd had their treats—she gave them all some attention and then looked up for the big guy again.

Rocket gave up his survey of her and had run to the front of the yard where he stopped and stood by the fence, staring at the car.

Not her car, but the car that had been parked in front of Ethan's house the last three days, the days she had been coming every evening to take care of the pets while he was out of town.

The sedan hadn't moved once, obvious because it was parked right in front of a cypress tree, keeping her from parking directly in front of Ethan's place, as she would have liked. It wasn't the same person parking daily—the car had not moved.

It got dark during the time she was here each evening. And leaving the place—with the dogs locked up again—made her nervous. Her fault. Truly and sadly, she was a chicken.

She let out a sigh of frustration. She had no problem doing a favor for a friend—even if it meant driving across town every day to make sure that her friend's pets were fed and let out for a few minutes on the days Ethan was gone.

But Ethan lived in Coconut Grove and parking wasn't always easy. He had just come down to the area a few months ago when he'd taken on his new job. And it wasn't that she didn't love Coconut Grove; she did. But the very beauty of the abundance of trees and bushes here also made it scary as hell at night. Ethan lived in a small duplex, so the space in front of the house wasn't large, and, granted, it wasn't private parking, but . . .

The house wasn't near shops or the night life that Coconut Grove offered and since it was part of a duplex, Riley didn't like parking in front of the offending car because she didn't want to take the space that someone else might need. Of course, she'd only be there thirty minutes or so, but still, Ethan's relationship with his neighbor wasn't great. The neighbor didn't like dogs or Ethan.

"Hey guys, what's not to like about your human, huh?" she asked the three little dogs milling around her feet for attention. Ethan was great. Six three, in great physical shape, blue-eyed, and with a sweep of pitch-dark hair that fell provocatively over his forehead. Right now, they were friends. Riley hoped that one day, they would be more. He teased and flirted with her when they were alone in the elevator at Suarez and Vincente, the advertising agency where he was an accounting executive and she worked as a concept artist. He liked to comment on her hair, calling her carrot-top even though her shade was a dark auburn, but then grinning and telling her that her eyes were a more beautiful green than any emerald. He also called her his, "Pretty young thing," and sometimes, his "Pretty young, sweet, little thing."

She was young, just twenty-three. But she was five eight. Not a giant, but hardly petite.

Ethan was good at his job, and he could be charming to clients and coworkers alike. But he was no doormat. She'd heard him lay it on the line to those who didn't comply with company rules. He could be hard—but only when necessary.

She smiled, remembering when he had hedged when she asked what was wrong, and he told her, "I need to be gone a few days. And I hate, hate, hate, having to send my dogs to the vet or the kennel." He'd grimaced. "Dog guy, here."

That, of course, just made him more perfect. She wondered sometimes if he knew how attractive he was, how . . . seductive. Then again, she knew that he appreciated her. But where did they take it from there?

Maybe he did just appreciate a really good friend. And she could be a good friend.

"Um, well, I couldn't just hang around at your place," she said, grinning, "but I could go feed them and let them out for you."

"I couldn't ask you to do that," he'd said quietly.

"You're not asking me. I'm offering," she'd assured him.

"Wow. Well, you are something, my friend."

"I don't mind."

"Still . . . hey, okay, think of it for you. What a thriller of a day! Driving extra and adding on to long work hours. It will be great!"

And she had laughed and assured him again. "You bet! A thriller! And, honestly, I don't mind."

That night, she'd come over to meet the dogs. And he'd watched her with admiration and respect and . . . more, she thought. They'd almost touched, almost kissed, and then . . . she'd left for the night, both suddenly a bit shy and maybe needing to get to the point where he wasn't going out of town and they'd have some time. Because if there was going to be something, it wasn't going to be a "thank you" for a favor or something that was just convenient. It was going to mean something.

"You are amazing," he had told her.

And the look he gave her told her that he found her amazing in many ways. And it was nice, allowing a nice excitement for the future.

Of course, it was true, she was an animal lover herself, so whether friendship grew into something more or not, she didn't mind watching the dogs. She just minded the car that kept her from parking directly in front of the gate—and hopped quickly in her car when it was time to leave.

This area was far from the little malls on the highway or the dozens of restaurants, bars, and shops that stretched through the center of Coconut Grove. She wasn't the bravest soul around. And while this area wasn't particularly noted for crime, it was a part of Miami and Miami-Dade County, and a city that size was never without its fair share of crime. Down by the bay, there were multi-million-dollar mansions and yacht clubs and more—but not far away, there were crack houses, too. A true mix of . . . just about everything!

"Okay, guys," Riley said, "I know, you like company and you like being outside, but I've got to get going now." As if she understood perfectly, Penny whined. She petted the dog's head. "Hey, I need to get some dinner, do laundry, and . . . well, hey. Hmm. Look at my sketches. I've done great drawings of you guys and just might do something more with them!"

Sitting there, trying to give the dogs time to run around before the darkness and the amount of foliage on the street made her too nervous, she started sketching. She had—if she did think so herself—some great puppy pictures. The three little ones posed together, Penny in a leap up into the air, and then her favorite, a sketch of Rocket, standing, staring out at the street, as if prepared to take on any unwanted visitor. Rocket was, beyond a doubt, a handsome dog—if not a warm and cuddly one.

"Okay, guys, in!" she said. Rocket usually listened to her command to return to the house.

Not that day. He was still staring at the car.

Riley walked over to the dog, setting her hand on his head. "Rocket, sorry, buddy, but I can't stay. Another two days and your master will be home and you can run around forever if you like."

The dog remained dead still, and Riley realized that he was sniffing the air.

Then she smelled it herself. There was an awful odor in the air.

Creepy. And she wanted to get away.

"All right, sorry!" she said firmly. She caught him by the collar. He didn't try to nip at her, but he struggled against her hold. Finally, she got him back to the house. The little pups ran on in—they knew there would be treats in their food bowls.

Rocket resisted another minute. But then he gave in.

Riley closed and locked the door promising, "I'll see you tomorrow!"

Darkness had fallen completely. A weak moon was struggling to show against a sky that seemed foggy and very dark.

She hurried out to her car, frowning as she noted that the trunk was ajar. She didn't believe that it had been so before, but she wasn't sure. And it didn't matter. She just wanted to get away. It occurred to her that the foul odor that was filling the night might be coming from the car—from the trunk.

She spun to get away from it, but she was in such a hurry that she tripped on her own feet and only caught herself from a heavy fall by landing on the truck of the offending car that had been parked in front of the gate.

She hopped back quickly, staring in horror, so terrified that she couldn't even scream.

It was dark. But there was enough light filtering through the hazy sky to show her that a body was stuffed into the trunk of the sedan.

A cloud lifted, as if on cue, and she could see that it was the body of a woman, partially clad, eyes still open in horror, a red slash across her throat and a spill of crimson around her as she lay trussed into a fetal position.

She still couldn't scream; she reached into her bag for her cellphone and keys, and she realized that she'd left them on the little table by the chair where she sat on the porch while letting the dogs run around.

In terror she turned, throwing open the fence, running toward the house as quickly as she could. Instinct insisted that she think logically. The car had been there for days.

Did that mean that the body had been there for days? That she was in no greater danger than she had been at any time while at Ethan's home.

Phone! Phone the police as she got the hell out!

She ran to the table where she'd left her keys and her phone.

They weren't there.

Panic seized her again. She could have sworn that she'd set both on the table when she'd gotten Ethan's keys out of her purse to open the door.

She dug insanely in her purse again, but her keys and the phone weren't there.

Ethan didn't have a landline.

For a moment she stood frozen. She still had the key to his place and at the least, she could have the dogs for company. She quickly opened the door, and they rushed back out, the little guys yipping happily, Rocket looking at her almost wearily, as if she'd finally got the problem.

And still . . .

She was terrified. Thinking desperately, she remembered that it was a duplex and whether the neighbor liked Ethan or not, he'd help her when he learned there was a body in a car. Wouldn't he? Wouldn't anyone?

"Okay, you guys stay here in the yard," she told the dogs. "I'll be right back!"

She headed out the fence to Ethan's part of the property, not glancing toward the still-open trunk of the car. Ten long steps brought her to the neighbor's side of the duplex, and she opened the gate to his part of the yard.

She ran up the walk to the front door. Like Ethan's, the door was beneath an overhang that provided for a little porch.

Riley started to knock on the door.

It creaked inward as she did so.

"Hello?" she called. "Hello?"

Lights were on in the house, but there was no reply. She could also hear a news anchor speaking on a television from somewhere within.

"Hey, please, I need help! Just to borrow a phone, just . . ."

She'd taken one step inside. And that was when she saw him.

The neighbor.

All she could think of was an old nursery rhyme, but a nursery rhyme based on the truth of something horrible that had happened.

"Lizzie Borden took an ax and gave her father forty whacks."

She didn't think that she'd ever known the man's name, though she had seen him a few times, coming and going. She'd always assumed he was in his fifties, a man with a thick head of white hair and trimmed beard to match. He'd stared at her when she'd tried a friendly wave, and she'd never seen him smile and still . . .

He lay on the couch. There was no ax in his head. But, like the body in the car, he had a red necklace around his throat and a pool of dark crimson beneath him.

"Oh, God, oh, God, oh, God!" she breathed, stepping out of the door quickly.

What if the killer was still in there?

She turned to run, not sure where to run. The house next door was dark. There were no cars on the road at all. But there had to be someone down the street.

Right.

Perhaps the killer.

No, the body had probably been in the car for days. And maybe this man had been dead for days as well. She needed to get it together.

The trunk had just been ajar tonight!

All right, all right, just walk down the street and find help!

But not alone.

As much as she hated running back by the sedan with the body, she raced back to Ethan's gate, let herself in, ignored the yipping little guys, and headed into the house for Rocket's leash.

It wasn't on the hooks by the door, and she cursed softly aloud, wondering where it might be. But it was as she stood there that she felt someone behind her and she turned, a scream welling in her throat.

This time, she found her voice.

"Hey!"

Spinning around in sheer terror, she was stunned to see that Ethan was standing behind her.

She threw herself into his arms, shaking.

"Oh my God, oh my God—thank God! Ethan, you're here, you are home!" she stuttered.

"Yeah, I was able to get back early. Grabbed a dial-a-ride and got here quickly. What on earth is the matter?"

"You didn't see?" she whispered incredulously.

"See what?"

"That car . . . that car parked in front of your house! Ethan, there's a body in the trunk."

He stared at her as if she had completely lost her mind.

"There's a body—in a car in front of my house?"

"And your neighbor is dead!"

"My neighbor? Ah, come on! He's not a nice guy, but he's not so bad that someone would want to kill him! Riley, I shouldn't have asked you to do this, I know how nervous you can get. There is no body in a car, and I'm sure that my neighbor is just fine," Ethan said.

He had such confidence and even a note of humor in his smile.

"Hey, you scared yourself into seeing things!" he told her. "Come on, sit down, I'll grab you a shot of whiskey and steady your nerves."

"Ethan, I'm not making it up! I walked outside and fell against the car and the trunk popped open. You had to have seen the body in it when you got here, oh, Ethan—"

"Hey, you pretty young thing. I did just walk by that car—jerk, parking like that in front of my place, but the trunk is closed."

"What? It was open. There's a body in it, I swear it. Rocket knew!"

"The dog knew there was a body in a car?" he asked skeptically.

"Ethan, I'm not crazy. I'm not terrified and seeing things. There is a body in that car and . . . go look!"

"Okay, but I'm sure the car is locked. And I'm not a cop, so I'm not going to break into that car, even if its owner is a jerk!" Ethan said.

He put his arms around her for a minute and pulled her close. "Riley, it's okay. It's dark and creepy around here at night if you're accustomed to this street. Maybe the owner is with a theater company and has a dummy or something, but . . . Riley, the trunk isn't open."

It was good feeling his arms around her. Ethan was good-looking, yes, but he was also strong and assuring. And right now, a bastion of strength against her terror.

"See? Let's walk outside and you can see that the trunk is closed."

She nodded and he turned to the front door, which was still ajar, pushed it open all the way, and stepped out. Riley hadn't noted that the little dogs were milling around their feet, wagging their tails, hoping for pets and affection, until she nearly tripped over one of them.

Rocket was still outside, standing in his guard position, but now watching the two of them.

"See?"

He was right. The trunk of the sedan was now closed.

"It was open!" she whispered.

"Riley, I think you might just be . . . afraid of the dark?" he suggested gently.

"Your neighbor!" she said. "Come on over with me!"

She headed out his gate, hurrying next door. He followed her. But when they reached the door—which had stood ajar when she'd come just minutes before—was now closed.

She hadn't closed it. She'd run out in panic.

She tried the knob. The door was locked.

"Riley," he said gently. "Honestly, I think that—"

"That I'm scared and seeing things," she finished. "But I'm not. And Ethan! My keys and my phone—I had them on the table when I was giving the dogs treats and letting them run around. They're gone. I mean, seriously, they couldn't just disappear."

"You checked your purse? You know, that bag you carry is like an endless cavern."

"No. I looked. Here!" she pressed her bag toward him. "You look! They're not in there."

He took her purse. "Wow! I'm being asked to see the personal inner sanctum of a woman's purse!"

"Ethan, I swear I'm not crazy."

"I didn't say you were crazy. But it is a crazy world. And it's easy to see what isn't there when you're afraid and it's dark."

She winced and nodded. "Please. Look. My keys and my phone aren't in my purse."

He took her bag and walked to the little table on the porch.

"Dump it! Go on!"

He did so. His keys were there; hers were not.

"Okay," he said gently. "They must be inside somewhere. You put them down when you filled the dog bowls or gave them water or . . . picked up poop. You are a good friend! More than a good friend," he said, smiling and smoothing back a lock of her hair.

"Well, with you here now, I'm not so terrified," she said, pausing to scratch a little pup's head. "Let's look inside."

"There you go. Good plan," he said.

They went inside and she walked into the kitchen, stepping on the clean puppy pads she had just put down and searched the counter.

No keys. No phone.

"Did you use the restroom?" he asked her.

She shook her head and hesitated, wincing. "I come in and let them out, put water in the bowls, put food in the bowls, check the pads . . . and head outside. I am a chicken and I know it."

"Did you go in any of the bedrooms? Turn the television on?"

"Ethan, I let the dogs out, I do what I need to do, and then go sit with them while they run around and I give them a few treats. I sketch for a few minutes so that they have a little time to run around and then . . . then I lock them back up and get out of here! The street here is dark. It's so funny, we're so close to so many places, and yet it's so quiet and dark here!"

"Okay, they have to be here somewhere," he told her.

He walked into the kitchen and then frowned, moving the giant bag of dog food that rested on the kitchen floor. The little pups didn't eat so much, but Rocket needed a lot of food.

"Hey!" Ethan said. He winced and picked up something beneath the bag.

It was her phone.

Crushed beyond recognition.

"Oh, man, that food bag is really heavy!" he said. "I am so sorry. But don't worry, I will get you a new phone as soon as possible. We can run out together after work tomorrow."

"Don't worry about the phone. I have insurance on it," Riley said, distracted. "How could I have gotten the phone under the food!"

"It probably fell out of your purse when you were setting it down to get the food. You don't leave it outside, do you?"

"No, of course not."

"Let's find the keys," he said.

She shook her head. "How could things have fallen out in different places? And Ethan, please, let's use your phone. We need to call the police!"

"For?"

"I'm telling you, Ethan, there's a body in the trunk of that car!"

"And you left your phone on the table outside?" he asked.

"Please?" she whispered.

"Okay, you sit down and calm down. I'll get my phone, and I'll call the police. But I'm going to tell them the truth, that you think you saw a body in a car and my neighbor's body in his house. Which is now locked. I'm not even sure that the police can break into a car or someone's home just because you think that you saw something."

Ethan took her by the arm and led her to the big comfortable sofa in his living-dining area, just to the left of the kitchen. He sat her down.

The front door was still open, and the little pups were standing on the porch then, watching them.

She saw Rocket too. He was standing a distance away, staring in at them.

"Rocket knows!" she whispered.

"Pardon?"

"Rocket. He was staring at that sedan. And I smelled something terrible—the corpse in it. Oh, Ethan, it's terrible! She . . . her eyes are open. She's like, like . . . tied at her wrists and ankles and squished into a fetal position. Her eyes are open. And she has a huge slash at her throat and . . . your neighbor. I kept thinking about the Lizzie Borden murders. He's lying on the couch and his throat is slit ear to ear, too, and I swear, Ethan, I'm not crazy!"

He sat next to her and set his arm around her, drawing a line down her cheek with his knuckles. "It's okay. I'm going to call the police. And we'll see what they can do."

She nodded. "Thank you," she whispered. And then she frowned and said, "Thank God you came home! You weren't due back—"

"I had to check on my folks. My dad is in a home, and they called and said that he wasn't well. I just had to sign papers and . . . I would have stayed longer, I meant to stay longer. But it's too painful. He doesn't know who I am."

"I'm so sorry. And your mom?"

"Well, as it turned out, my mom wasn't there. She couldn't take it either, I guess. I went all the way home and found out that she flew up to New York to stay with her sister. Anyway, I can't do anything, and Dad has a companion now at this place that he really likes and they're both happy just listening to Elvis tunes all day. So . . . I came home."

She nodded. "Fate, destiny! Thankfully, you came. I was going to head out to a neighbor's house—I couldn't go home! I didn't have keys or a phone. But . . . you came."

"Fate, destiny," he said, and smiled. "Okay, let me do this!"

He smoothed her hair back once again and stood, pulling his phone out of his pocket. He dialed and spoke, repeating everything that she had told him.

He listened.

He gave the address to the officer at the end of the other line, and then explained again, saying that it seemed someone had closed the trunk and then locked the door to the other half of his duplex.

"No, I'm not crazy!" he said angrily to the phone, glancing at Riley and wincing. Then he sighed and said, "No. No one is in any immediate danger. All right then. Thank you."

He ended the call and looked at her.

"They think I'm crazy."

"Well, you can tell them that I'm the crazy one!" she said.

"They're coming, but I could tell that it didn't sound like any kind of an emergency to them."

"Two dead bodies—and it's no emergency," Riley said. She tensed, sitting up and whispering, "Ethan, do you think . . . could there be anyone in the house with us?"

He grinned and then indicated the three little pups who had made their way through the open door to gather around Riley's feet.

"They may not be big and vicious, but they bark like crazy. And, hey, that big dude out there, Rocket. He'd be barking his head off."

"But still . . ."

"Riley—"

"I know! I know that you think I'm crazy and the police may think that I'm crazy too. But, Ethan, someone could have closed your neighbor's door and it may have an automatic lock. And anyone could have slammed down the lid on the trunk of that sedan. And—"

"Hey, okay. You sit tight. I'll check out the bedrooms and the bathroom."

"No!" Riley said.

"But—"

"I don't want to sit tight. I'll come with you!" she said. "Don't you ever watch horror movies? It's when people split up that they wind up in trouble."

"Have you been watching too many horror movies?" he asked her.

"I don't watch them at all anymore!"

He grinned. "Okay. Come with me. That will be fine."

Riley stood quickly, nodding.

"Get behind me now!" he told her.

"Oh, you bet!"

"And, hmm, let's see . . . wait. Right here, I'm not going anywhere, I'm just heading into the kitchen."

She stood watching him as he walked into the kitchen, drew open one of the drawers by the sink, and pulled out a carving knife.

"Forewarned is forearmed," he said sagely. "And now, I'm armed!"

"Great. Except that you think I'm crazy."

"Still, what if you're not?" he said lightly. "Forewarned is—"

"Forearmed. Let's do it!" Riley said.

She inched behind him as he headed into the first bedroom through the small hallway behind the living room. He opened the door, and she waited nervously as he turned on the light.

It was his bedroom. There was a large bed there with a handsome headboard, medieval cover, and plump pillows. Two sets of dresser drawers were in the room as well.

And a closet.

She reached out for him, but he was gone as he headed across the room to the closet, throwing the door open.

Nothing. Nothing but neat rows of his shoes and hangers filled with his work shirts and jackets.

"Next room," he said.

The second bedroom had been turned into his office. Again, she tensed as he opened the door, and turned on the light.

His desk and computer were in the center of the room. There were a few chairs lined up against the far wall.

"Closet again!" he whispered.

Once again, he walked ahead before she could grab him.

But this closet held luggage, boxes, and miscellany.

No killer lurked within.

"Bathroom," he said.

She nodded and they left the second bedroom/office to return to the hall and open the last door there, that led to the bathroom.

He turned on the light.

Just the usual. Toilet. Sink. Medicine chest. Toiletries.

But a shower curtain was covering the bathtub. Again, Riley felt tension fill her as Ethan stepped forward and wrenched the curtain back.

"Nothing."

"See. We're safe. And the police should be here soon," he said.

They walked back to the living room and Riley noted that the door was still open.

"And we're both idiots!" she said. "We left the front door open."

"Riley, I have four dogs. Three little ones who yap like crazy and one big one capable of ripping a throat out."

"Right. Of course."

"Come on. Sit down. Chill for a minute!" he said. "I'm going to fix you a drink."

"I'm good. Really. I don't want the police to come and smell my breath and think I'm not just crazy but drunk too."

"Okay, then, come sit!"

He made a sweeping bow, indicating the couch. She smiled and stepped ahead of him and took a seat. She leaned back and groaned.

"My keys!" she whispered. "We still haven't found my keys."

"We will find them," he assured her. "And, by the way, thank you!"

"For being crazy certain I saw murdered people?" she asked.

"For taking care of these guys."

"Of course."

"We really are more than friends!" he whispered.

She touched his cheek. "I would have done it no matter what."

"But you do like me."

"I—uh, yes," she said honestly.

He slid an arm around her, smiling. "I like you too. And I don't really care to be careful anymore, I mean, you know, because we're coworkers." With his free hand, he stroked her cheek.

Riley smiled, thinking that this was something she had so wanted, and yet today . . .

She wasn't crazy. And she hoped the police could prove that!

She frowned suddenly. "Ethan, what did you do with your bags? We need to get them if you left them outside somewhere."

"Oh, they're not outside."

"You said that you got a ride. Where's your car?"

He smiled again, stroking her cheek, leaning toward her. "I did get a ride."

"Then . . . shall I pick you up for work tomorrow? Oh, wait, I can't— unless we find my keys. No, I have a second set. Of course, I'll have to get a locksmith to get into my apartment, but . . ."

"I won't need a ride," he said quietly.

"Why is that?"

She had never seen such a strange smile on his face before.

"My car is right out front," he said.

"Your car?"

"The sedan is my car. The sedan—with the body in the trunk," he said.

Her heart seemed to stop. He had to be teasing her. Teasing her for her imagination, for being such a coward, or for being, in his mind, crazy.

"Come on, Ethan," she said. "The cops are taking their time getting here, right? We should start looking for my keys again. I mean, they have to be here somewhere. I got here, right?"

"You don't have your keys," he told her. "You won't find your keys."

"Ethan—"

"I'm kind of sorry," he said. "I mean, you are good to take care of animals like this for a friend, but . . . well, you are a pretty young thing, and you're . . . well, like I said, you are awesome, in so many ways, and I have wanted you for a long time—ever since I first saw your young, beautiful face."

"Ethan, what are you talking about?" Riley was suddenly scared. Of Ethan! This couldn't be. It was a macabre joke.

"Pretty young thing, pretty young thing!" he murmured. "I love pretty young things, beautiful ones like you . . . the kind who are, no pun, a thriller! I just love them a very special way, I love the slick feel of a woman's life's blood against her skin, and I love to look into her eyes when that blood drains away . . ."

"What?" She shrieked in horror and tried to jump to her feet.

He pulled her back.

"Ethan, the police will be here any second—"

"No, they won't be here any second, Riley. Oh, come on, please, I guess I am a pretty good actor. You fell for that!"

He held her arm.

But not her mouth.

And this time, she screamed with sound. And the sound was a loud and terrible shriek that seemed to reverberate through the air and even shake the walls of the house.

And she screamed again as he pushed her down, crawling over her.

He still held the carving knife. The carving knife he had taken—presumably for protection for the two of them!

And he smiled that macabre smile at her as he raised the knife over her.

She screamed and screamed again. He slammed the hand that held the knife over her mouth to whisper to her.

"God, are you beautiful! The terror in your eyes. The feel of your skin." He paused to smile. "I couldn't help it. I had to pretend to leave. I wanted you to see the body in the trunk, see my neighbor! I have dreamed of this since I left New York. Well, I had to leave. You might have heard of the women who had been stabbed there, and the blond, well, she died beautifully, but my neighbor . . . that was all for you, all to see the beauty of fear in your eyes, all to see your face as you realized that I was about to kiss your beautiful lips when they were covered with blood, touch your skin, feel you, love you . . ." Again, he paused to grin. "It is a thriller, isn't it?" he queried.

She managed to draw a grunt of pain from him as she bit down as hard as she could on his hand. He almost dropped the knife. She kicked him, kneed him with all her strength. He cried out in pain, but told her, "Oh, baby! Nothing like a woman who puts up a big fight and screams loudly, no whimpering!"

She screamed. "They'll get you! Oh, yes, I heard about the murders in New York. But I have screamed and screamed. Police will come!"

He appeared amused, still confident. And she'd hurt him, yes, but again . . .

He was straddled over her, tightly now, lest she tried to kick again.

She was going to die. She'd been seduced, in love, and even as she stared at the sheen on the knife, she couldn't believe that a man so perfect . . .

Could be a heinous killer.

He was smiling, smiling, and his smile was horrid, and he was suddenly hideous to her, because, of course, he was her murderer.

And now, worse. Behind him, she saw that Rocket had come into the house. The huge dog was staring at them strangely, as he tended to do.

Ethan's eerie grin deepened.

She was going to be stabbed to death and ripped apart by the giant jaws of the dog!

She screamed again, the sound loud, and long, and shrill, and still she knew there was no hope as she waited for the pain of the blade to fall.

Except . . .

It didn't.

The sound that followed her scream was like something straight out of hell, a growl, a rumble, something so deep that it, too, seemed to shake the air.

And to her amazement, there was a whir before her, and Ethan was ripped away from her and he was suddenly on the floor.

Rocket.

His own dog.

Maybe dogs did know the difference between simple right and simple wrong.

Ethan was shouting and the dog was standing over him, teeth gnashing.

And she realized, Rocket wasn't going to rip apart her flesh, he had saved her life!

Riley tore out of the house, screaming desperately, heedless of the darkness, heedless of the brush and the trees and the shadows and even the darkness of the night.

She stood in the road screaming and people began to pour from their houses. A woman tried to help her and more people arrived as she spurted out her story.

The police came quickly.

And there was a body in the trunk of the sedan.

The neighbor was found dead as well.

Ethan was found only half-dead. Rocket had stood over him, threatening to rip out his throat, until the police arrived and took him in.

Riley never found her keys. Nor did she spend that night at her apartment. She went to her sister's house. Her brother-in-law had been in the army and still had his service weapon. It was a good place to be. Safe, secure, and where she was loved.

In the days to come, she discovered that there were several unsolved murders not just in New York, but in the other two cities that the man had lived in during the past several years.

He was under arrest but taken to a hospital ward. And it was while he was there that he ripped out his IV and tried to escape that a doctor, defending himself and the nurse Ethan had tried to use as a hostage, ended his reign entirely with a well-placed needle into his heart.

Riley was numb on hearing the news. She had thought she had known a man. Worse, she had been attracted to him, and he had been a psychotic killer. She wasn't sure she could trust her judgment anymore.

Except on one thing.

Her brother-in-law told her that Ethan's dogs had been taken to the pound. That brought her to life again. She hurried there and was glad to hear that the little fluffy mutt pups had been adopted.

But not Rocket. He was still there.

He watched her gravely as she walked up to his cage.

"You are man's best friend!" she told him softly, hunkering down to pet him through the cage.

Could a dog nod? She thought that he did.

"My best friend!" she assured him. "Like I said, there are those who think that dogs are best, best all around. Better than people. And now, that may just be true in my life!"

And, later, having legally adopted him and leaving with Rocket on his leash, she thought that she had lost one friend, one friend who she had ridiculously thought might be more.

But she had gained an amazing friend as well. One she would love the rest of his life and her life, which, thanks to him, promised to be much longer than it might have been.

Bringing the dog home to her own apartment in the Kendall area, she watched him sniff, test his new bowls, and make himself at home.

Maybe because of what had happened, and most probably because of Rocket, she wouldn't be such a terrible chicken again. She would be far more careful and make sure that she knew people very well before trusting them.

And still, she had a true friend. He lay at her feet, and she patted him on the head and scratched his ears.

"Rocket . . . well, he said it would be a 'thrill.' But Rocket, the thrill now is knowing you! And yes, pup, you can sleep on the bed as long as we both shall live—a long time now, most probably, and all thanks to you!"

WILLIAM KENT KRUEGER

BEAT IT

"Beat it," Mrs. Helgerson said with growing impatience. "Just beat it."

Dwayne stood before the dark green chalkboard, staring at several poorly erased words ghosting up from behind a film of chalk dust. In each hand, he held a black, felt eraser.

"Do it now, Dwayne," Mrs. Helgerson said.

Dwayne lifted his hands and slapped the erasers against the board, leaving two white rectangles on the surface. He stared at them, imagining they were empty graves dusted with snow.

"Oh, for pity sake," Mrs. Helgeson said. "Knock them together."

They were alone in the classroom. The other kids had gone home for the day. Mrs. Helgerson stood at the back wall, near the door to the coat room, where she was pinning Thanksgiving drawings from her sixth-grade students—turkeys, mostly, but there were a few pilgrims in the mix. Dwayne's drawing wasn't among them. The sheet of manila paper he'd handed in had appeared to be blank. When Mrs. Helgerson questioned him, he'd told her, "My turkey doesn't want to get eaten. He's hiding."

Dwayne eyed the two erasers, and once more slapped them against the chalkboard. This time the two chalk rectangles reminded him of coffins made of white pine.

"I said knock them together. Like this." She pantomimed what she wanted, bringing her hands together with a clap.

Dwayne eyed the erasers in his hands, then slapped them together in an explosion of white dust, which he breathed in. He coughed hard while he watched the dust settle onto the floor at his feet.

Mrs. Helgerson rolled her eyes. "Do that at the window, Dwayne, so that the dust stays outside."

Mrs. Helgerson's exasperation was clear in the pitch of her voice, but Dwayne didn't mind. Most of his teachers had been like Mrs. Helgerson. Either they spoke to him sharply or they tried to ignore him altogether. Mrs. Helgerson was better than some. At least she was pretty, and she always smelled nice.

He walked to the window and slid the pane up. It was late November. The weather in Bigelow, Texas, had cooled enough for the windows to be closed and the radiators filled with hot water from the boiler in the basement. Ollie, the janitor, had once let Dwayne put a shovelful of coal into the furnace that heated the boiler, and Dwayne had watched the coal turn to flame as hot as an August sun on his face. All the other adults in the school had to be called Mister or Missus, but the friendly janitor had given Dwayne permission to call him Ollie. Some of the kids made fun of Ollie because he was a janitor and had to clean up the mess when one of the littler kids peed on their desk chair or someone threw up all over a bathroom stall. But Ollie never said a bad word about the kids whose messes he dealt with.

The sixth-grade classroom was on the second story of the old schoolhouse. From the window, Dwayne could see the dark silhouettes of the Guadalupe Mountains pressed against a vast blue sky. He put his arms out the window into the cool air and clapped the erasers. There was no wind and the dust drifted slowly down toward the dead grass of the schoolyard below.

Behind him, he heard the classroom door open, but he didn't turn around. He had a job to do.

"Oh. I thought you'd be alone."

Now he turned. Mr. Carraway, the school principal, stood in the doorway, his hand still on the knob. His eyes shifted from Dwayne to Mrs. Helgerson, then back to Dwayne.

"Dwayne's done," the teacher said. "Aren't you, Dwayne."

"I haven't finished my job yet."

"Beat it, Daryl," Mr. Carraway said.

"My name's Dwayne."

Mr. Carraway glanced at Mrs. Helgerson. "He's big for a sixth grader."

"Held back," Mrs. Helgerson said. Then added, "Simple," and tapped the side of her head.

"Like I said, Daryl. Beat it."

"I'm supposed to clean the erasers. It's my job. Everyone has a job. Some kids are safety patrol. Some kids are hall monitors. Some kids pass out papers. Some kids pick up papers. I clean the erasers."

"He wanted a job too," Mrs. Helgerson explained to the principal. "So today I gave him one."

"They're clean enough," Mr. Carraway said.

"Not yet." Dwayne stepped to the chalkboard and slapped one of the erasers against the surface. This time the chalk image reminded him of an empty raft on an empty sea.

"I said beat it, Daryl."

"The erasers," Dwayne said.

"Are you too stupid to understand a simple directive?"

"It's my job," Dwayne tried to explain. "Mrs. Helgerson gave it to me."

Mr. Carraway took a deep breath. "Tell you what, Daryl—"

"My name's Dwayne."

"I've got another job for you. The erasers in the science classroom need to be cleaned. I'll give you a dollar to clean those erasers."

"A dollar?"

Mr. Carraway drew a leather-tooled wallet from this back pocket and plucked out a bill. He held it toward Dwayne. But as the boy moved to take it, the man pulled the dollar out of reach. "You only get this if you do a really good job cleaning the erasers in the science room. Is that clear?"

"Yes, sir."

"Good. And don't come back here. You've got another job to do now, one you're being paid for. Do you understand, Daryl? When you're finished, just go on home."

Dwayne took the dollar. His Aunt Rose gave him an allowance of a dollar a week, which he was saving so that he could buy her a nice Christmas present. He'd been thinking maybe a soft bath towel. The ones Aunt Rose had were thin and scratchy.

Dwayne placed the erasers on the sill of the chalkboard. He didn't feel good about leaving them still full of chalk, but he'd accepted money for another job. And Mrs. Helgerson didn't seem to mind.

"Close the door on your way out, Daryl," Mr. Carraway said and turned toward Mrs. Helgerson.

Dwayne stepped into the hallway, then reached back for the knob.

"Not here," he heard Mrs. Helgerson say. "He might find us."

"Relax. I've given him work that'll keep him busy a good long while."

"Lock the door," Mrs. Helgerson said. "Just to be sure."

Dwayne closed the door and a moment later heard the lock click behind him.

He descended the stairs to the first floor and turned down the hallway toward the science classroom. The school felt completely deserted. He'd never been in the schoolhouse before when it was so quiet. He liked it this way. Usually there were kids and noise and bells and shoving and sometimes mean things that were done to him that made other kids laugh. He thought about the final image the eraser had left in chalk dust on the board, an empty raft on an empty sea. He thought that wouldn't be so bad, to be alone on your own raft on a sea where no one bothered you.

He heard the squeak of rollers on the linoleum of the hallway. When he turned, he saw Ollie, the janitor, pushing a cart mounded with rugs. He liked Ollie, who was one of the few people who didn't make Dwayne feel stupid. The janitor was tall and lean and reminded Dwayne of the trunk of the oak tree in Aunt Rose's backyard that offered cool shade in the heat of a summer day. Ollie spotted him and lifted his hand in a wave.

"Hey there, Dwayne. A little late for you to be in school, isn't it?"

"I have a job," Dwayne said. He walked to where Ollie had paused with the cart. He put his hand on the mound of rugs. "What are you doing?"

"Remember that dust storm last week?"

"Do I ever. Aunt Rose and me had to sweep for hours."

"Can't just sweep these rugs, Dwayne. Got to knock the dust clean out of 'em. I'll do it outside."

"How?"

"Come on, I'll show you."

Ollie pushed the cart to a door at the end of the hallway, which opened onto a ramp that led down to the playground in the back of the school. The janitor jingled as he walked, the result of a big ring of keys that hung from a belt loop on his pants. Ollie had told Dwayne that on the ring was a key to every door in the schoolhouse. He wheeled the cart across brittle grass to the steel jungle gym, where he lifted the top rug and draped it over one of the horizontal bars. He reached to the bottom shelf of the two-tiered cart and came up with a long wooden paddle. The paddle had several holes cut in the blade.

"Step back, Dwayne," Ollie cautioned. When the boy had done as he was asked, the janitor said, "Now watch this."

Ollie drew the paddle back and swung, just like Dwayne swung a baseball bat. Dwayne never had much luck hitting a ball, but Ollie's paddle slammed against the rug with a great *thwack*! A cloud of dust and grit exploded from the rug and settled on the ground.

"Want to try it, Dwayne?" he said.

He held out the paddle and Dwayne took hold. It was heavier than he'd imagined, heavier than any baseball bat he'd ever held. He gave Ollie a doubtful look.

"Go ahead. Beat it," Ollie encouraged him.

But Dwayne still didn't swing.

"Designed that rug beater myself, Dwayne. See those holes I drilled? They make it what you might call aerodynamic. Don't worry," Ollie assured him. "You'll swing like a champ."

Dwayne grasped the paddle with both hands, took a stance as he might have at home plate, and swung with all his might. The paddle connected to the rug with a loud *thwack*, eliciting a cloud of grit and dust, just as there'd been when Ollie himself had swung.

"Well, done, Dwayne." Ollie gave him a pat on the back, and Dwayne grinned from ear to ear.

"All right, son. You'd best get to your work." Ollie took the paddle from Dwayne, then said, "By the way, what's this job of yours?"

"Mr. Carraway gave me a dollar. I have to clean the erasers in the science room."

"That so? A dollar, eh?"

"I'm saving money to buy Aunt Rose a soft towel for Christmas."

"Well, Dwayne, that's just about the nicest thing I ever heard. Did you tell Mr. Carraway what you'll do with the money?"

Dwayne shook his head. "He was busy with Mrs. Helgerson."

"What's that?"

"He had business with Mrs. Helgerson."

A darkness came over Ollie's face. It reminded Dwayne of when the dust storm had swept in and blocked out the sun and afterward everything was dirty.

"Go on to your chore," Ollie said.

Dwayne left him and reentered the school building, which was still empty and quiet. He went to the science room, where there were two chalkboards, one along the wall at the front of the room, and one along the wall opposite the row of windows. On one of the boards was a drawing of the upper part of a person's body and head. A kind of pathway led from the person's mouth to the stomach. Beside the drawing were written the words "Alimentary canal." Which made Dwayne smile. It was comforting to know that teachers made mistakes, too. Even he knew how to spell elementary.

There were four erasers, two for each chalkboard. He went about his business, sliding a windowpane up and clapping the dust from the erasers in the air outside. To test his work, he slapped the erasers against the dark green chalkboards. He wanted to do a good job for the dollar he'd been paid, and he took quite a while to be sure all the erasers were free of dust. He tested them again and again. They made a loud sound like the paddle had made when he beat the rug. *Thwack! Thwack! Thwack!* So loud, in fact, that he thought he could hear it echoing in the hallway outside. When the erasers finally left not a hint of ghostly chalk dust, he knew he was finished and was proud of himself.

Although Mr. Carraway had told him to leave when he'd finished, Dwayne mounted the stairs to the second floor and returned to Mrs. Helgerson's classroom. He wanted to tell them about the good job he'd done. When he reached the room, however, he remembered that Mrs. Helgerson had told Mr. Carraway to lock the door. He looked through the glass pane but didn't see them. He knocked, but no one answered. Finally, he tried the door and was surprised to find that it was unlocked.

When he stepped inside, he thought the adults must have finished their business and left. He was a little disappointed. He was proud of himself and wanted to share that. He was about to leave when he saw the spill of red paint on the floor of the coatroom at the back of Mrs. Helgerson's classroom. He'd spilled milk in the coatroom once, from the thermos in his lunchbox, and Ollie had cleaned up the mess with a mop and bucket. Dwayne figured Ollie would have to come again to clean up the spilled red paint.

He walked to the coatroom to confirm his suspicion. And there were Mrs. Helgerson and Mr. Carraway, sprawled naked on a rug on the floor. Staring at their smashed skulls, he realized that the red spill wasn't paint.

He needed to tell someone. He needed to tell Ollie. He raced from the classroom, down the stairs, and outside to the playground. A rug hung over the monkey bars, the same one he and Ollie had beaten with the paddle. And the cart was still there, but Ollie was not. Dwayne thought about Ollie's office in the basement, and he turned and ran back into the school.

The basement, like the hallways above, was a long corridor. The rooms off to the sides were used to store school things—desks and chairs and empty aquariums and gym equipment, and also the cleaning supplies and machines Ollie used in his work. The furnace room was there as well, and next to it, the janitor's office. Dwayne had been to the basement many times, where Ollie had shared with him all these subterranean mysteries.

He went straight to the janitor's office. A brass plaque was affixed to the wall next to the door. The plaque read "Custodial Office." Beneath that was the name "Oliver Helgerson."

Dwayne didn't find Ollie in his office. But as he stood there, trying to think what to do next, he heard a soft wailing come from the furnace room next door. When he stepped into the doorway of that room, he found Ollie standing before the furnace, which heated boiler water for the radiators. The door of the big furnace was wide open. In the janitor's hand was the rug beater, covered in blood. Ollie was staring into the furnace. Dwayne could tell that he had added a shovelful of new coal to the fire inside and the flames danced high and hot.

Ollie turned toward Dwayne. In the firelight, the boy saw the glisten of tears streaming down the man's cheeks. This was the first time Dwayne had ever witnessed a grown man crying, and it broke his heart to see his friend in such misery.

As Dwayne watched, Ollie threw the bloodied paddle into the furnace and shut the door. He turned to Dwayne and wiped at the tears. "Our secret?" he said quietly.

Dwayne thought a moment. It seemed to him that he and Ollie were both rafts on an empty sea now, and when this idea came to him, he didn't feel so alone.

"Okay," he said.

"Thank you, Dwayne. You're a good kid. Best if you just beat it now."

And so he did.

NEIL S. PLAKCY

BILLIE JEAN

"You know that sometimes I need a woman to be by my side at events," Alex Reyes said, his Cuban accent making the words seem gentle, as we unloaded lumber from the trunk of my lime-green Chevy Bel Air. "The rules in Miami in 1968 are not as strict as those when I was growing up in Cuba, but they exist."

"That's a beard," I said, intentionally making my voice a little rougher. It wasn't hard; I came from working class stock on Maryland's eastern shore, about as different from his private boarding school in New Hampshire as possible.

He looked at me. "Really? Where do you hear terms like that?"

I simply looked back at him. We had met at a gay bar a few months before, though at the time he was using the location as a cover for an anti-Castro group. "Oh," he said. "The Cockpit."

The bar was located out near Miami airport, so the name had a dual meaning. In the afternoon, it attracted airline employees who needed a pick-me-up before heading to work, or those on quick layovers. By nine o'clock, the clientele had transitioned to gay men who put different meanings on the words "cock" and "pit."

Alex was slim and darkly handsome, with black curls he kept

tamed with a pomade that smelled like bay rum. That day he wore a plaid shirt with the Brooks Brothers hanging sheep crest on the pocket, and Levi's blue jeans. A couple of the buttons on his shirt were undone, displaying a few dark curls of chest hair I longed to run my fingers through.

But we were not at his house in Coral Gables to play—at least not yet. He wanted to build a wooden fence around his property, primarily to protect his driveway from the prying eyes of his neighbors, and I had volunteered to help.

Earlier that morning, we had laid out where the fence would go so we knew how much lumber to buy. Alex lifted one of the fence posts and carried it up close to the stucco side wall of his house.

"You were telling me about your beard," I said, as I followed him, with a sledgehammer we had rented from Poe's on US 1, where we'd bought the lumber.

"It was a dinner on behalf of the Historical Society." Alex carefully positioned the post in the dirt, and then reached for the sledgehammer.

"Probably easier if you take that expensive shirt off first," I said.

He unbuttoned the shirt, revealing a skin-tight white sleeveless T-shirt beneath it that hugged his pecs and his flat stomach. He hung the shirt off the branch of a mango tree, and I gave him the sledgehammer.

His arm muscles rippled as he raised it over his head and slammed it into the top of the fencepost, which sunk into the loamy Miami soil.

"Her name was Billie Jean, and she came here from Atlanta, where she was a debutante, to work in the bank in my building. A young woman whose family I knew in Cuba works there too and she introduced us." He smiled. "When I picked her up that night, she looked like a beauty queen from a movie scene."

While Alex fiddled with the post, I fetched another from the pile of wood on the driveway. He moved a couple of steps away from the house and positioned the next post.

He managed investments for his wealthy Cuban exile family and others in similar circumstances, from a high-floor office overlooking Lincoln Road in Miami Beach. "I met her a few times at the elevator, and we chatted."

"Flirted," I said.

He raised the sledgehammer and slammed it into the post.

"I wouldn't call it that," he said.

"But I would," I said. "I've seen you in action. Your voice purrs, you blink those long eyelashes, you stare steadily into a young woman's face."

"Are you jealous?"

"I'd rather have you stare at my ass than my face," I said, turning that body part toward him as I fetched another post.

"But what a handsome face it is, my George," Alex purred. He was turning that same charm on me, and my dick rose to the occasion.

"Enough flattery. Let's get this fence in place so we can go inside, strip down, and cool off."

It was early spring in Miami, one of the best seasons. The sun was not too bright, cooling breezes came in from the ocean, and most of the snowbirds and tourists had left.

We worked for a few minutes, measuring and placing posts. "What about this girl?" I finally asked.

"She came to see me yesterday." He wiped sweat from his brow in a move that excited me, watching his tanned skin ripple. "She announced that she is pregnant. And that I am the father."

"What?"

Alex didn't answer, just motioned for another fence post. And though I had only been dating him, if you want to call it that, for a few months, I knew I had to let him speak in his own time.

"I am not, I assure you," he said. "I have not slept with a woman since I was seventeen, a prostitute my uncle purveyed for me in Havana."

"Did you tell her that?"

"Of course not. I do not care to share my personal business with her. To do so would certainly open me to further threats." He slammed another post in and we moved to the street edge of his property.

"She says that I brought her here after the party, made love to her, and impregnated her." He frowned. "But I have an alibi for the evening."

"Excellent. Bring that person forward and you destroy her credibility."

"It's not so easy," he said.

I looked at him, sweat running down his white undershirt, pooling under his biceps and his armpits, and felt a wave of longing through my body. At the same time, I knew what he was saying.

"You were with a man after that dinner," I said.

He nodded. "You."

We did not talk again for a while. We measured, and I took my turns with the sledgehammer, slamming the posts in. I was angry at this woman, for threatening Alex, and angry because even if I spoke up, ruined my own reputation and his, no judge would believe us anyway because we were homosexuals and couldn't be trusted.

We installed the posts all the way to the driveway. Alex had bought beautifully carved wooden gates, but they needed special hardware, and he finally accepted that the job was beyond the both of us. "I will call my cousin Carlos later," he said. "He runs a construction firm. He can finish the job for me."

His house was a single-story in the Spanish hacienda style, with coral tile roofs and arched doorways. It was constructed as a square, with a central courtyard. You entered from the front door into a lovely living room that led directly into the open courtyard, shaded by palm trees. In the center was a small pool with water lilies, and when the water evaporated it cooled the air around it. The eaves all around the house were deep, keeping the hot air out, though Alex did have a window air conditioner in his bedroom.

The kitchen was to the left, and to the right was what had once been a dining room but which Alex had remodeled as a home office. His bedroom and the master bath were directly across the courtyard from us.

We walked through the courtyard, pulling off our undershirts as we did. When we got to his bedroom we both kicked off our shoes and socks and dropped our slacks. Then we went for each other with a wild passion, our sweaty bodies slipping and sliding together.

———

When I came out of the shower, Alex was reclining naked on the bed, reading the *Miami Herald*. I picked up his slacks from the floor, straightened them out, and removed his wallet. Then I laid the pants carefully over the chair by the door.

I crossed the room to him, feeling the terrazzo tile beneath my bare feet, and handed the wallet to him. "Give me a dollar," I said.

He smiled at me. "I think what we just did was worth more than that."

I kicked him in the shins, and he barked. "I want you to hire me to investigate this Billie Jean."

"You can do that?"

"According to my private investigator's license from the state of Florida."

"I mean, because we're . . . involved."

I felt foolish, standing there naked explaining my job to my lover, but I persevered. "When I take on a case I look for evidence of what's true and what's not. You say you never slept with this girl, and I believe you. But someone did, and if I can find out who, I can get you off the hook without explaining what you and I were doing while Billie Jean says you and she were making a baby."

Alex opened his wallet, a soft leather made from pampered Swiss cows and burnished by craftsmen with centuries of expertise. He pulled out a single bill. "You're sure this is enough?"

"To create a contract between us. I'll bill you for expenses."

He gave me Billie Jean's full name and her address, and after some time spent comfortably in his bed, I drove over to her apartment, in a modern building on Tigertail Avenue in Coconut Grove, the hamlet nestled between Coral Gables and the city of Miami. It was an area rich in local history, shaded by towering oaks, the streets lined with brilliant hibiscus and bougainvillea.

I had no idea if Billie Jean was home or not, and only the sketchiest description of her, but if she was the kind of young woman I thought she was, she'd be going out on Saturday night. I thought I might observe her from a distance before I jumped into any further research.

At about 7:00 p.m., a dark sedan pulled into the building's parking lot, and stopped in front of apartment two on the first floor—the one where Billie Jean lived. Her Lothario beeped the horn with two quick toots, and a moment later she stepped out of the doorway.

I was sure it was her. She had a blond bouffant, as Alex had described, and she carried herself like she was in a pageant. She wore a blue long-sleeve blouse, with a single button open at the neck. Over it she wore a black-and-yellow plaid dress, with a kind of yoke front. It stopped several inches above her knees, and she wore black high heels and pantyhose.

She swung easily into the car. After a moment the driver backed out and turned onto Twenty-Seventh Avenue heading north. I followed at a sedate distance, keeping the sedan in view but letting other cars stay between us.

We crossed US 1, leaving the leafy hamlet of the Grove behind us, and moving into the commercial outskirts of Miami. The road was lined with hardware stores and drugstores, and increasingly the signs were in Spanish as well as English. Because of the three balls in front of a sign that read *Casa de Empeño,* I figured it was a pawn shop.

As we got closer to the airport, I wondered if Billie Jean was on her way somewhere. But she hadn't carried any luggage, just a small square purse in a blue that matched her blouse.

Miami Senior High School loomed to the right, and we kept on going, past tiny cafés and laundromats and bank branches. By the time we crossed Flagler Street, the main east–west artery in the city, we were deep in Spanish-language territory. With their increasing prosperity, the Cuban immigrants who had begun arriving in 1959 with the rise of Fidel Castro had left run-down apartments on South Beach and were moving to the suburbs.

Ahead of us I saw the overhead lanes of the Dolphin Expressway. There were no cute marine mammals in sight, just lanes of heavy traffic heading both east and west. I had no idea where the black sedan was going, so I stayed in the middle lane on Twenty-Seventh, hoping the sedan would continue northbound.

At the last moment, however, the sedan swerved into the left land and caught the last flash of a yellow light onto the westbound ramp.

I was stuck in the middle lane at the light, and all I could do was watch the sedan climb the ramp and disappear.

Well, I hadn't expected much from the night, so I wasn't that disappointed. I managed to get into the right lane and took the Dolphin all the way to the MacArthur Causeway, which led me home to Miami Beach. I had a couple of hours to grab dinner and relax before I had to be at my part-time job as a bouncer at the Cockpit.

It was a busy night, and I had to eject several rowdy drunks, so I didn't think about Alex and his Billie Jean problem until the next morning. I decided I'd take a drive over to Coral Gables and see if I could coax Alex into going to brunch with me, and then perhaps back to his house afterward.

When I got there, though, there were two carpenters in white pants and white T-shirts building the rest of the fence, and Alex was in his driveway hosing down his car, which had gotten splattered with mud somehow.

I didn't want to stop at Alex's while he had workmen there, especially ones who might report back to his cousin. At thirty-two, Alex was well beyond the age when his family thought he should marry, and he didn't want to give them any inkling of his true nature.

So I went to the Holsum Good Food Restaurant on Dixie Highway for a southern-style Sunday breakfast. As I ate my grits, biscuits with sausage gravy, country fried steak, and scrambled eggs I tried to remember the details of the car I'd been following the night before. Was it a

Mercedes, like Alex's? I'd only noticed that it was a dark color—was it a deep black, or a more faded color?

I didn't want to consider that after complaining about his problem to me, Alex had decided to take matters into his own hands. I couldn't think that. Alex was a good man, dedicated to his family and his country. He'd always been kind to me, and I'd never seen him act in violence.

I, on the other hand, had grown up around angry voices and raised fists, so I had built my body up to protect myself and others. I had spent years in the Navy exercising justice, compelling obedience. Alex was the gentle moon I was drawn to like the tides. I couldn't lose that opinion of him.

I worked the afternoon shift at the Cockpit, which was quiet, and then went home by myself. The next morning I started my research on Billie Jean Taylor at the bank.

I wanted to verify that the girl I'd seen on Saturday night really was Billie Jean. But I was out of luck—none of the tellers had that name in front of them. I remembered that Alex had been introduced to her by a Cuban girl, and I went up to a teller whose nameplate read Maria Luisa. She looked the most Cuban, with voluminous dark hair, tan skin, and bright red lipstick.

"My favorite teller isn't here this morning," I said. "Billie Jean?"

"She didn't come to work this morning," Maria Luisa said. "Can I help you with something?"

I patted my jacket pocket. "Shoot, I left my deposit at the office. I'll come back." Another customer quickly took my place.

My next step, I figured, was to check on Billie Jean. Had she left town? Maybe she was blackmailing someone else, and she'd taken his money and run.

I drove to Coconut Grove and was surprised to see a couple of police cruisers around Billie Jean's building, and the door to apartment two propped open. Fortunately, I saw an officer I knew.

When I was in the navy, almost every guy I met was off limits, for one reason or another. Miami Beach, though, was another story. Guys were attracted to my rough exterior and my muscles, and I took some stupid risks. One of them involved me nearly getting arrested for indecent exposure.

Then the cop, Officer Mike Hunt, got a good look at what I was exposing, and he half-dragged me to a building under construction in downtown Miami, where we took care of business together. Since then we'd become acquaintances of a more professional nature, and I parked and walked over to where he stood. "What's up, Mike?"

"Hey, George. Couple of guys on bikes riding through Shark Valley yesterday afternoon discovered a body. Turns out to be the girl who lived here, in apartment two."

"You know her name?"

"Billie Jean Taylor. You know her?"

I shook my head. "I know a pair of stewardesses who live in the building, that's why I stopped."

Mike accepted that and stepped over to a couple of young guys who were peering in the driveway. While he was occupied I slipped back to my car.

I drove back over the causeway to my office on Washington Avenue above Mr. Ho's Chinese restaurant. They were already firing up the wok for lunch, and the smell of sizzling pepper steak and pork fried rice filtered up through the walls.

While I waited for the bank to close at three thirty, I worked on a report for a regular client, an insurance company. On this case, I'd followed a man who claimed disability benefits based on a car accident, but I'd snapped photos of him driving and lifting heavy debris around his yard.

Around three fifteen I walked up to the building where both Alex and Billie Jean worked, though fifteen floors apart, and staked out a spot on a planter in the shade of the building. Eventually the employees filtered out, and I could tell a couple of the young women had been crying. That was good for me; it meant they already knew what had happened to Billie Jean.

I lit a cigarette and watched the young women. When Maria Luisa came out of the building, I caught her eye and smiled.

My approach worked, and she sat down beside me. "You have one of those for me?" she asked.

I was disappointed it was my cigarettes she was after rather than my face or body, but you take what you can get.

"Sure." I held out my pack of Marlboros and she took one, and then I lit it for her. "Rough day?" I asked.

"How can you tell?"

"You've got a bit of mascara at the corner of your eyes. Looks like you've been crying."

She took a drag of her cigarette. "I really should stop these. They're supposed to be bad for you."

"Most things we like are."

She laughed. "I guess you're right." She peered more closely at me. "Didn't you come in this morning, looking for Billie Jean?"

I shrugged. "She always charms me. I like to look for her when I come in."

"Well, she's not coming in anymore." She took another drag. "The police came by the bank this afternoon. They found Billie Jean's body yesterday. In the Everglades of all places."

"She wasn't the nature type?"

Maria Luisa next to me shook her head. "Not Billie Jean. The only exercise she liked was on the dance floor." Another drag. "And on her back."

She put her hand up to her mouth in a display of false modesty. "I shouldn't say that."

"Why not? Won't hurt her feelings," I said.

"She was a sweet girl, really. Fresh out of finishing school, called herself a Georgia Peach. We bonded because we both have double names."

I cocked her head and looked at her. I was trying not to reveal anything.

"My parents named me Maria Luisa," she said, with just the hint of a Spanish accent. "But in school everybody called me Mary Lou. I thought that was more American, anyway. When I met Billie Jean we bonded over that."

"Cute. Mary Lou and Billie Jean," I said. "She had a lot of boyfriends?"

"If you can call them that. She liked to date but she didn't want to get tied down." She leaned in close to me. "I'll tell you a secret, though."

I smelled the tobacco on her breath. "What's that?"

"She was about to get tied down permanently. She was pregnant."

"That happens, when you have sex."

"And when you don't take precautions," Mary Lou said. "I would never go to bed with a man without him using a condom. And even then, I clean myself up real good afterward, washing away all his cooties."

She laughed. "At least that's what they told us to do in high school."

"Was she going to get married, Billie Jean?"

Mary Lou blew out a deep breath and stubbed out her cigarette. "She had a list of men who might be the father and they all turned her down flat. A couple of them offered her money to get it taken care of, and she took the cash but didn't do anything."

"Did you tell the police all this?"

She nodded. "But Billie Jean never told me any names so I couldn't say much. And you know, I didn't want to seem like a gossip." She laughed. "And here I am telling everything to a total stranger."

"I've got one of those faces," I said. "People like to confide in me."

She stood up. "Well, I hope the police can find out who did this. Billie Jean wasn't the ripest banana in the bunch, but she was all right, and she didn't deserve to die."

She walked away, and I saw her meet up with a couple of her coworkers at the bus stop on Alton Road. She didn't look back at me. But I noticed that she didn't get on the bus when it came. An orange Camaro pulled over at the corner and stopped, and the driver beeped the horn.

Mary Lou looked into the open window, then got inside and they drove away.

Since I was there at Alex's building, I walked over to a pay phone and dialed his office number. I'd been to his office a few times, where I'd been introduced as to his secretary as a business associate who managed a couple of properties Alex's firm invested in.

So I was comfortable addressing her by her first name. "Hey, Lourdes, it's George Clay. Is Mr. Reyes available?"

"Hold one moment please."

"George? Have you found anything out?"

"Is this a good time? I'm downstairs."

"Sure. Come upstairs."

Alex ran his own firm, but he shared the office space, and Lourdes's time, with a couple of older Cuban men, who mostly seemed to smoke cigars and talk on the phone. I didn't want to show up at his office frequently enough to arouse suspicion. It was bad enough in their eyes that he was associating with an Anglo, although we were acceptable business subordinates.

"What have you found?" Alex asked, when I was seated across from his broad mahogany desk with the door closed behind me.

"Good news and bad news," I said. "Billie Jean is dead."

He gulped. "Is that the good or the bad news?"

"From our point of view, it could be either. Where were you Saturday night?"

He shifted in his chair. "At home. After you left I took a nap, made myself some dinner, and then watched television."

Maybe the police would accept that as an alibi, but I wouldn't. Alex never "watched" television. He might have it on in the background, but he was a book reader.

"After I left, I went home and took a nap, too," I said. "I guess we wore each other out." He smiled, and then I went in for the kill.

"But around seven, I drove over to Billie Jean's apartment building on Tigertail in the Grove. I watched her come out of her apartment and get into a black sedan."

I watched him closely. His lips were slightly parted, and the rest of his body was tightly coiled. "The license plate was muddy so I couldn't make it out. But I followed the sedan all the way to the Dolphin Expressway, when I lost it. The driver was heading west, toward the Everglades."

Alex didn't say anything.

"I went over to your house yesterday morning to tell you about it, but I saw the guys working on your fence. And I saw you washing your car."

He nodded. "I like to do that on Sundays. You know that."

"I do. Yesterday morning, a couple of bicyclists found Billie Jean's body out by the Shark Valley bike path. No sign of that dark sedan with the muddy license plate."

It finally clicked. "Are you accusing me of murdering her?" he said indignantly.

I sat back in my chair, though I desperately wanted him to deny it. "Well, you have to admit the details match. You have a shit alibi, a dark sedan with muddy plates, and a motive to get Billie Jean out of the way."

"I can't believe you of all people would think me capable of something like that."

"I don't," I said. "But you're going to need a better alibi for the police than you were watching TV, which I know for a fact you never do. Where were you?"

His shoulders sagged. "I can't tell you."

I leaned forward and my voice was almost a growl. "You can suck my dick but you can't tell me where you were on Saturday night?"

With his mouth open, he looked like a fish that had just been caught and dragged out of the water. "I tired you out on Saturday afternoon, so I don't think you were with another man. Were you?"

"Absolutely not."

"Then you were with your buddies. The ones from the Cockpit." I leaned forward. "You have to be honest with me, Alex. I don't give a fuck about your politics. You could be planning to overthrow Castro for all I care. But I don't want to see you go to the electric chair for a murder you didn't commit."

"Just three of us," he said. "At Alfonso Padron's house."

Something about that name clicked. "The guy from Brigade 2506?" That was a group of men the CIA had recruited in 1960 to raid the

Bay of Pigs on the island's south coast and try to foment a revolution against Castro. It had been an abysmal failure, yet the men responsible were still lauded in Miami.

"You see why I don't want to have to explain."

"Well, you may need to."

His phone rang, and he held a finger up to me and answered. "Yes, Lourdes, put him through."

I listened as he verified that he was Alex Reyes, and then answered a series of questions with yes. "I'll be there," he said, and he hung up.

"That was a detective Pinder from the Miami Police Department. He asked me if I knew Billie Jean."

"To which you answered yes," I said. "I heard that much."

"He wants me to come in tomorrow morning to help with their inquiries." He leaned down and put his head in his hands. "George, what can I do? This will ruin me."

"First of all, you don't know what they know. They were at the bank this morning, and I know they spoke to your friend Maria Luisa, or Mary Lou if you prefer. She must have told them that you and Billie Jean went to that Historical Society dinner."

He suppressed a sob.

"But you weren't her only gentleman friend," I said. "I spoke to Mary Lou myself this afternoon, and she implied Billie Jean was a slut."

He looked up at me. "But she had such a sweet appearance."

"Who knows, some men may find that appealing. The point is, your name is probably not the only one Mary Lou gave up. There may be a whole list of them. If you were the only one, the police would have come upstairs as soon as they finished at the bank."

"Maybe you're right."

"Of course I am. This is what I do for a living." I tried to be calm, though inside I was raging at whoever had killed Billie Jean and put Alex into this position. "Though I have to say, for an ordinary guy, you have a lot of secrets. Who you sleep with, who you don't sleep with, the guys you hang out with, and what they're plotting."

"We are planning a demonstration," he said. "At the Ermita de la

Caridad in Coconut Grove."

"The church?"

He nodded. "It's a very potent symbol to the Cuban people. The statue inside, the Virgen de la Caridad, was smuggled out of Cuba in 1961. Our plan is to stage a demonstration asking her to bless our efforts to topple Castro."

"You don't have to tell the police what you discussed at Padron's house. Just that you were there, having a couple of glasses of rum and sharing cigars with some old friends."

"But the police will want to confirm with Alfonso. What do I tell him?"

"That a woman you dated has been murdered, and the police need to eliminate you from their inquiries. That's all." I forced myself to smile. "Your pals will tease you but it adds credibility to your playboy image."

He sat back against his leather chair. "I can do that."

"The more important question is what kind of evidence the police have. If they have better suspects, they'll stop there. But they may need to check your car for fingerprints. They may have castings of tires from the area."

I thought very carefully about what I wanted to say next. If I phrased this wrong, Alex could toss me out of his office and our relationship, such as it was, would be over. And if I phrased it correctly? I might not get the answer I wanted.

"Alex," I began. "I have a lot of respect for you. The way you've faced the challenges in your life, the way you carry yourself through the world. The way you treat other people." I took a deep breath. This was harder than I had expected. "And I have a deep, personal feeling for you. Not just when we are having sex, but whenever I think of you."

Alex looked at me with curiosity in his eyes. "Are you saying you love me, George Clay?"

"I wasn't raised to believe that love was possible between two men," I said. "But being with you is changing my mind."

When I was a teenager, my friends and I found a swimming hole beside a steep cliff. We had challenged each other to dive off it, and though my heart beat a mile a minute and my arms and legs felt like jelly, I did it.

"Yes, Alex Reyes, I believe I love you."

His eyes were like dark pools, as deep as that old swimming hole. Then he smiled. "Good, because I believe I love you too."

Such declarations are usually accompanied by some physical action, at least in romance novels. But I had something else to say.

"Tell me honestly. Will the police find any evidence that Billie Jean was in your car, or that you were out in the Everglades Saturday night?"

It seemed like I waited a long time before Alex said, "The only time Billie Jean was in my car was over three months ago, when I took her to the Historical Society dinner. And if I recall, she wore white gloves that night. So there should be no fingerprints in my car. She came up here once, last Thursday, after her shift was over at the bank, to present her demands. Lourdes will verify she was here."

"Then you need to tell the police that. Why did she come up here?"

"Why, to . . ." Then he stopped. "You want to know what I would tell the police."

"Yes. On the one hand, it would be better not to tell them about the blackmail, because that gives you a motive. But on the other hand, if they already know, and you lie, that puts you in deeper."

"I will have to think about this." He stood up. "It's almost quitting time. Can I buy you a cocktail?"

There were innocent restaurants where Alex and I could have gone, as two male friends sharing a drink. But we were both so accustomed to hiding that we went to his home instead. The fence was up, protecting prying eyes from noting the regularity with which my lime-green car appeared, and Alex could be counted on to have a selection of excellent rum, the kind that was so good you sipped it from small cups and avoided mixers.

At Alex's house, Cuba libre was a motivating force rather than a drink.

Once we were settled comfortably in his living room, our shoes off and our shirts opened, I said, "I have a feeling that there's more to Billie Jean Taylor than I understand at present. Tell me everything you know about her."

"It isn't much. I know her family must be wealthy, because she made her debut with the Atlanta Debutante Society at the Piedmont Driving Club."

There was a lot to break down in that single sentence, but Alex saw my confusion and explained. "The Piedmont Driving Club is very high class, exclusively white and Anglo-Saxon. Even with all my father's money I'd never be invited to play there. Very patriarchal, and the women are relegated to a servant role—except for the debutante ball. She went to a very fancy private school in Buckhead, the rich neighborhood of Atlanta, and apparently spent a lot of her high school years preparing for the ball, learning to dance and how to behave."

"So what's a girl like that doing slumming as a bank teller in Miami Beach?"

"I asked her that, though not in so many words. She said her parents were pressuring her to marry a boy back home who she didn't care for, and she was trying to get out from under that expectation. Her father's a banker in Atlanta, and he knew someone in Miami who got her the job."

He sipped his rum. "Her parents have been expecting her to get this independence out of her system and come home and do what's right. But she had no intention of doing that."

"And she confided all this to you on one date?"

"Well, I heard part of it from Mary Lou, when she fixed us up. I asked Mary Lou to go with me to the Historical Society dinner, but she said she was dating a very jealous Cuban boy and he wouldn't let her. She suggested Billie Jean instead."

"And why do you think she and Billie Jean were friends?"

"Back in Havana, Mary Lou's family were wealthy. Her father and his brothers owned a small bank that loaned to the sugar cane industry. When Castro nationalized those companies, the bank failed and Mary Lou and her family came here. Her father drank himself into an early grave and the family's almost out of money, except for what Mary Lou and her brother Omar earn. He's a mechanic at a garage in Allapattah, near where they live. The antithesis of their father, who was a genteel man who always wore a guayabera and smoked the best cigars. Omar is a thug. But he looks after Mary Lou and their mother, so I can't criticize him."

"Both Billie Jean and Mary Lou are bankers' daughters, working behind teller windows," I said. "I guess that could make them friends."

We talked some more, drank some more good rum, and then went to bed. Before I drifted off to sleep I wondered if Billie Jean had other friends, and my answer was no. If she had anything to confide, she'd turn to Mary Lou. And Mary Lou wasn't the type to spill everything to the police.

Tuesday morning I did some searching on her. People believe, probably from what they've seen on TV, that private eyes can operate outside the law, but they're wrong. Most of what we do is plain old shoe leather and using public resources. I knew that Mary Lou's last name was Bustos, and that she lived in Allapattah with her mother and brother. An Omar Bustos had a phone listed on NW Twenty-Fourth Court.

I drove over there. It was a run-down neighborhood of single-family homes and small apartment buildings. A woman in a housecoat stood outside the address I had, listlessly trimming a rosebush. She was probably only fifty, but she looked older, her hair uncombed, her back stooped. When she thought no one was looking she took a swig from a flask in her pocket.

As I drove back to the beach, I wondered if Mary Lou was part of Billie Jean's attempt to embezzle money from Alex Reyes. Her family looked down on its luck. She might have suggested her rich friend as a good target. If I went back far enough, maybe she had introduced Alex to Billie Jean as a potential rich date.

I went back to my office and did some work for a few hours, then shortly before bank closing I parked on Alton Road just south of the bus stop and waited for Mary Lou to arrive.

This time her ride showed up before the bus, though once again it took a beep of the horn for Mary Lou to recognize that the driver in the brown Datsun was there for her. She hopped in, and I followed. I figured that her ride might be taking her home.

I was thus prepared for her driver taking a sharp left onto the Venetian Causeway, a low-lying series of bridges that linked Miami Beach to the mainland via a bunch of small islands. Her driver knew the city; he zigged and zagged through a series of local roads underneath the hulking mass of the new I-95 highway and past the VA Hospital.

I believed I knew where he was going, so I was able to keep a few cars between us. Eventually he pulled up in front of the address I had for Mary Lou.

I had planned to ambush her at home and see what else she could tell me. But on an impulse I followed the brown Datsun, curious to see who was chauffeuring her around in a variety of vehicles.

It didn't take long. The Datsun turned north on NW Twenty-Seventh Avenue, into a neighborhood of factories, marine supply operations, and warehouses. A couple of blocks later the driver pulled into a garage, and neatly slotted the Datsun into a waiting area on the side.

When the driver got out, I saw he was wearing overalls, and he hurried to the garage's bay. Most likely Omar Bustos. By then I had to keep moving with traffic, but I circled around and parked in the lot of a Cuban bakery, facing the garage.

It was a busy place, with a set of gas pumps out front and along the side street, two bays with car lifts, and a side area used for washing. A sign read that a wash was complimentary with any service under fifty dollars, while a service over that price got you an exterior wash and an interior detailing.

The next car up for the wash was a dark Mercedes sedan. In the daylight, I recognized it was a few years older than Alex's. And the license plate was still obscured by mud, though a skinny guy in a tank top, shorts, and flip-flops was about to take care of that with a hose.

The pieces fell together. Omar Bustos had access to a variety of cars through the garage. There was a solid chance he had picked up Billie Jean on Saturday night in the Mercedes he'd borrowed, then driven her out west on the Dolphin Expressway.

From there it was a simple jump to him killing her and leaving her body at Shark Valley. But whatever evidence might be in that Mercedes was about to be obliterated by the exterior wash and interior detailing.

I spotted a phone booth half a block down the street and hurried over there. I slotted in my dime and called Alex Reyes. "Listen to me carefully," I said, when he answered. "I need you to call the police detective you spoke with. Tell him that you drove over this afternoon to see Mary Lou Bustos at the garage where her brother Omar works, and you spotted a car a lot like yours there. You remembered that Omar and Billie Jean dated briefly, and you're worried that Omar might have killed Billie Jean and is destroying evidence by having that car cleaned."

"Hold on, I'm writing this down," Alex said. Then he repeated it to me.

"Let me give you the address," I said.

"You don't need to. Omar services my car there."

I hung up and walked back to my car. The kid in the flip-flops had moved the dirty Mercedes from a spot by the wall to one near a hose. As I watched, he sprayed the car down with water, then attacked it with soap-laden cleaning cloths.

I wasn't so worried about the exterior of the car, though it would add credibility if the license plate was still mud-spattered when the police arrived.

I drummed my fingers on the roof of my car. If the police arrived. I hadn't waited at the phone booth for Alex to call back. What if he hadn't been able to reach the detective on the case, or convince him?

I had to do something to slow things down. I walked across the street and approached the kid doing the washing. "Hey, you do this kind of wash without service?" I asked, pointing to the sign.

"*No hablo Ingles*," he said. He kept scrubbing.

I dug around in my basic Spanish vocabulary. I'd been practicing with the kid who delivered for the Chinese restaurant downstairs, who was from El Salvador, not La China.

"*Este lavado, sin servicio?*" I asked.

This time the kid stopped. "*Si. Diez dólares.*" He opened the car door, which was just what I didn't want him to do, and began miming all the things he would do to detail the car. "*Buen valor,*" he said. "No?"

"*Si, buen valor,*" I said. Out of the corner of my eye I saw a police car approaching on NW Twenty-Seventh Avenue, red and blue lights flashing. I thanked the kid and went back across the avenue to my car, where I watched what was happening from a distance.

The uniforms were there to keep the kid from his detailing work, and a few minutes later a plain-clothes detective pulled up in his own car. He spoke with the kid, and then with Omar Bustos, and eventually the Mercedes was towed away by a police truck.

The owner wasn't going to be happy about that.

I was at work at the Cockpit that night when Alex called there for me. The bartender motioned me over to the phone.

"Mary Lou and Omar Bustos just pulled up in front of my house," he said in a voice so low I had trouble hearing him. "I was in the living room, and I heard them arguing outside. I think they know I told the police about Omar."

"Don't let them in," I said. "I'm on my way."

I made my apologies to the bartender and dashed for my car. The Cockpit is on the edge of the city of Miami, far enough from downtown that the cops don't usually bother us, and so it was only a quick ten-minute drive to Alex's. It felt like forever, though, my heart beating fast as I darted around slower drivers and zoomed through yellow lights.

The orange Camaro I'd seen before was parked on the street in front of Alex's house. I jumped out of my car and felt under my seat for the baseball bat I kept there. I had a license for a gun, a sweet little revolver, but I didn't carry it to the Cockpit, so it was locked up at my office.

I approached the house stealthily. Fortunately the fence gate was brand new and recently oiled, so it didn't make any noise as I swung it open. I heard loud voices from inside the house. I should have called the police before I left the Cockpit, but I'd been in such a rush to help

Alex that I forgot.

I was on my own, then.

I moved up to where I could look in one of the living room windows. Alex was standing on the terrazzo floor, bleeding from a cut to his forehead as Omar Bustos wrapped a leather belt around his wrists. Mary Lou stood to the side, holding a small gun aimed at Alex, but her hand shook.

I circled around the house to the back, where a sliding glass door led to Alex's bedroom. With the point of my knife, I made quick work of the lock and slid it open.

It wasn't as well-oiled as the gate and it squeaked, but I was far enough from the action in the living room that I didn't care. I was in the house.

I could hear Alex arguing with Omar, so I knew he was still alive, but I didn't know what they wanted to do with him. As I looked around Alex's bedroom, I spotted an oil painting of his family's *finca*, or ranch, back in Cuba. There was a safe behind it.

If Omar and Mary Lou wanted money, that's where Alex would take them. But would he be stubborn enough to resist giving them anything?

I crept to the bedroom door and looked across through the courtyard. Alex was facing my way, and his head jerked up when he saw me. I pulled out my wallet and grabbed a couple of bills and waved them, and he nodded slightly.

I could hear him by then. "I have a safe in my bedroom," he said. "Cash in there, and bearer bonds. You know what those are, Mary Lou."

"Whoever holds them can cash them," Mary Lou said. She said more to her brother, in rapid Spanish, and Alex, who was following the conversation, agreed, nodding eagerly.

Omar walked out into the courtyard, and I stepped back into the shadows of Alex's bedroom. I heard the three of them walk over the cobblestones, past the bubbling of the fountain.

"Everything is in the safe behind the picture of the Finca Clara,"

Alex said.

A hand reached in and flipped the overhead light on, and the palm-frond ceiling fan began to move lazily. I was behind the door, considering my options. Omar was the strongest threat, but Mary Lou held the gun. If I knocked her brother out, she could shoot me or Alex.

"Give me the gun, *hermana*," Omar said, "and then Alex, you tell her how to open the safe."

It was the opening I needed. As soon as Mary Lou handed the gun to Omar, I came out from behind the door and slammed the baseball bat into his midsection as if I was aiming for a ground ball. All those years of Little League back in Maryland paid off, because Omar fell backward, and the gun flew from his hand.

Mary Lou and I both dove for it, but I elbowed her in the chest, grabbed the gun, and rolled up to a standing position. With my right hand holding the gun, I untied the belt around Alex's hands.

Mary Lou knelt over her brother crying as Alex called the police. One of the great things about a small, wealthy enclave like Coral Gables is that a police car was there within minutes. Two uniformed cops took custody of Omar and Mary Lou and called for backup, and quickly Alex's small house was filled with men and women in uniform.

A Coral Gables detective took me and Alex into the kitchen separately to tell our stories. I worried that they might try to delve deep into the relationship between Alex and me, and why he'd called me rather than the cops. And that was one of the first questions that Detective Leonard asked.

"I'm a private investigator, and Mr. Reyes hired me to investigate a blackmail threat against him. He knew that I was nearby, working a second job."

The police finally left Alex and me alone in his living room. "How did Mary Lou and Omar know who called the cops to the garage?"

"Omar saw an Anglo talking to the car wash boy a few minutes before the cops got there. He described the guy to Mary Lou, and she put two and two together. She saw you at the bank, asking about Billie Jean, and then she spotted you heading to the elevator. She figured out you were working for me."

"And they came here to confront you? Or ask for money? Why did you let them in?"

"I didn't have a choice. They played me. Omar held his gun to Mary Lou's head and said he'd shoot her if I didn't let them in."

He sighed. "Apparently Omar was the only man Billie Jean slept with who was careless, so when she confronted Omar with the pregnancy, the three of them cooked up this blackmail scheme. But once they connected you with me, they knew they had to get as much money as possible and then get out of town pronto."

"Do they know about you?"

"You mean that I prefer men? It didn't come up, though I'm sure if Omar knew he would have added *maricón* to the other insults he tossed at me."

"But they must have known that Billie Jean didn't sleep with you. Of all the men on her list, why target you?"

"Billie Jean only targeted men who kept accounts at the bank, because she was going to snare a rich husband. When she got pregnant, she used those resources to target me, among others. From what Mary Lou said, I am the wealthiest of Billie Jean's paramours."

"And probably the only one who didn't stick his dick into her. There's irony there."

"But she had evidence that I was with her at the Historical Society dinner. And she was a white girl, and I'm a Cuban. People will believe what they want."

He slumped back against the sofa. "But she went too far. She started threatening that if Omar wouldn't marry her, she'd get Mary Lou fired from the bank. So the two of them picked her up last Saturday night, took her to the Everglades, and shot her."

He looked up at me. "Omar was even brandishing the pistol, saying it was the same one he had used on Billie Jean."

He began to weep, and I moved over next to him on the sofa, put my arm around him and let him rest his head on my shoulder.

"Originally they were going to hold me overnight and take me to the bank in the morning. But then I saw you and I told them I had money in the safe."

"We make a good team," I said.

"And what did you tell the police?" I asked.

"The truth. Billie Jean said I was the one, but her kid was not my son."

DAVID R. SLAYTON

HUMAN NATURE

She lay too still in the little square, green glass sparkling around her skull like a halo.

Andrew held his breath, stepped to her, crouched, but paused midreach. He knew better than to touch a body, but he felt for a pulse anyway.

Nothing, which didn't surprise him. A lot of blood had mixed with her hair and the wine from the broken bottle.

He didn't scream for help.

In summer, Mykonos Town would be full of light and tourists, but on a winter night the white-washed buildings, the too-blue shutters, and the stone streets felt like an empty stage. It felt like somewhere Andrew didn't belong.

Hands shaking, he dialed 112 and spoke in broken Greek, explaining what he'd found to the operator on the other end.

"Do you speak English?" she asked.

"Yes," he gasped.

"Where are you?"

Alex backtracked to find the signs, always hard to spot in the maze of little streets and gave his location.

"Stay there," she said. "They're coming."

She hung up without saying goodbye.

Andrew couldn't take his eyes off the dead woman. He was used to ancient bones and dirty fragments, not to bodies, not to people.

Turkish tobacco, more acrid than American, more noxious, pricked his nose. Who smoked anymore? It seemed a dying habit, even in Greece.

Andrew hugged himself and wished he'd worn something other than a polo.

He'd gone out for Eighties Night, telling himself that the food at the beachside taverna was better than the one closer to his hotel, that the walk was good for him, but he'd really just wanted to see Marco.

Andrew knew the bartender only flirted with him for the tips, to not take it seriously, but the attention relieved his boredom. There were only so many books or so many translations he could work through after the long days at the dig site.

The police arrived in a crowd of stiff, dark uniforms, looking more like the military than what he was used to back in Chicago.

The middle-aged officer who approached him had an impressive mustache and serious brown eyes.

"Did you touch her?" the cop asked. Andrew didn't know how to tell his rank, what the bars on his shoulder meant, but his tone said that he was in charge.

"Did you touch her?" the cop repeated.

"I tried to take her pulse. I told the operator that."

"You're the American."

"Yes," he said. "One of them. I'm with the University of Chicago."

"When did you arrive?"

"A week ago."

The guy wasn't writing anything down. Was that good or bad?

"By ferry or catamaran?"

"Ferry," Andrew said, though he wasn't certain what the question had to do with anything.

He'd been tempted to pay for the faster boat. They'd found a grave on Delos, and Andrew had the honor of excavating it, a perk of having Edward Miller for a mentor.

The other cops had started photographing the body.

"Why are you here?" the cop demanded, waving at the square. He loomed over Andrew.

"I was going to the taverna," Andrew said. "I wanted something to eat."

"They said there was a tourist on the island."

"I'm not a tourist. I'm with the University of Chicago."

"Do you have your passport?"

"Not on me," Andrew said. "It's in the safe at the hotel."

The cop's eyes narrowed.

"Which hotel?"

"The Electra."

"You said you weren't a tourist."

"I'm not, but the Electra gave me a great price since it's the off season. I have my passport card and my university ID."

Andrew didn't reach for his wallet.

Mykonos was supposed to be gay friendly, but that was in summer, not when the little streets were so dark, so lifeless—not when he could just disappear into the water without anyone ever knowing where he'd gone.

"Show me," the cop said with an impatient gesture.

Moving slowly, Andrew took out his wallet and handed over the cards.

The cop glared at them like they'd done him wrong.

"Did you see anything?" he asked, passing the cards back. "Anyone?"

"Just her," Andrew said with a gesture at the too-still form.

The cop scanned the alleys, his eyes fixing on one in particular, but Andrew couldn't see anything of interest.

"Who would do this?" he asked.

"We've had word of thieves on the island, artifact thieves. You should be careful, Doctor Patras."

Andrew swallowed.

"You can go. We'll be in touch if we have questions."

Andrew hurried off but glanced back when a camera flash drew his eye.

They'd turned the dead woman over.

Andrew didn't know her name, but he recognized her. She'd been in the taverna the last time he'd gone for dinner, her laugh a little too loud, her leer a little too suggestive as she flirted with Marco.

Andrew's appetite vanished and he headed back to his hotel.

———

He took the morning boat to Delos and spent the day sifting dirt and cataloging the grave's upper strata. They'd break through soon, but he had to go carefully. Whatever lay below, with the body, might be a prize worthy of a museum, but the upper layers were full of ancient debris and just as important to their research.

Andrew blinked away the orange-purple sunset on the ride back to Mykonos and tried to shake the memory of the dead woman, of her laughter and what his mother would have called bedroom eyes. He thought of Marco and hoped his own interest wasn't as blatant.

"Are you going to spend the night on the boat?" Edward asked, bringing Andrew back to the moment.

Andrew hadn't even registered that they'd docked.

"What's got you so preoccupied?" Edward asked, climbing the ramp, hand gripped to the rail to steady himself against the rocking ferry. "That inscription? Or is it James Dean?"

Andrew's face warmed. Edward's nickname for Marco wasn't unfair.

Marco had the movie star looks, even if he bore no resemblance to the dead actor.

"I was thinking about the woman they found," Andrew said, taking up his messenger bag and climbing off the ferry.

It felt strangely personal to be the one who'd stumbled across her body.

Edward shook his head.

"Julia," he said.

"You knew her?" Andrew asked as he followed Edward toward the town.

"She was with Berkley. I don't know what she was doing here. Their current dig is at Nemea. Maybe she was just trying to get away from all of it."

Edward waved his hand like he did when lecturing, an invitation for his students to ask follow up questions.

"Away from what?" Andrew asked.

"She had a son, Samuel—Sam. He was special needs." Edward's face bent with sadness. "He died last year."

"That's horrible."

"It is. Her husband stayed in the states to raise him so she could come here."

"Were you close to her?" Andrew asked.

Edward made a so-so gesture with his hand. He liked to play the grumpy professor, but he was more sociable, and more of a gossip, than he'd ever admit.

"I heard that the cops think there are thieves on the island, that they're looking for antiquities," Andrew said.

"That's a constant, but Julia wouldn't have anything to do with it." Edward scoffed. "No. No. She was with *Berkley*."

Andrew smiled at his mentor's passionate defense. He never could think poorly of a colleague.

"Who would kill her?" Andrew asked.

"I don't know," Edward said. "The last time we spoke we talked about regrets, the things she wished she'd done, like spending more time with her son. Life is too short, Andrew."

It was, Andrew decided.

"I'll see you tomorrow," he said.

"Tomorrow," Edward agreed.

Andrew turned toward the taverna.

A few old men gathered on the patio, beneath the lattice that grape leaves would cover in the summer. They smoked and ate a long, early dinner.

They'd likely be there all night. The Greeks enjoyed leisurely meals, a habit Andrew could find endearing when he wanted to relax and annoying when he was in a hurry.

He tossed the men a polite *yassas* as he passed.

Inside, Marco leaned over the long wooden bar and gave Andrew a smile that he couldn't quite read. Marco looked happy to see Andrew, but hadn't he been the same with Julia?

A tight black tee revealed a V of golden skin dusted with hair. Marco had just a bit of a beard and dark curls.

"You didn't come by last night," Marco said in accented English.

"Something happened," Andrew said, stepping closer.

"The lady in the square."

"How did you know?" Andrew asked.

"It's a small island," Marco said with a shrug. "Smaller in winter."

The taverna felt cavernous now, but it would bustle in a few months. Andrew had no doubt that he'd have little of Macro's attention then.

Andrew wondered how he survived in the meantime, without the extra tips.

Music drifted through the space, Michael Jackson singing about loving a certain way.

"I thought last night was Eighties Night," Andrew said.

"Every night is Eighties Night," Marco said. "You like this music?"

Andrew didn't want to cause offense by saying it felt dated, that it took him back to his parents dancing in the kitchen of their little house in the Chicago suburbs. Those were good memories, he decided, before the cancer, before he'd lost his dad.

"Yeah," he said. "I do."

"Then you should come every night." Marco beamed, reached for a wine glass, and nodded for Andrew to sit. "At least every night I'm working."

Andrew smiled and sat.

"You want food?" Marco asked, replacing the cork on a green, glittering bottle. "Your usual?"

Andrew should eat. He tended to forget to when he was hyper-focused on his work. Had that been Julia's mistake, too much wine on an empty stomach?

"Yeah," Andrew said. "Please."

It was nice that Marco already knew his order. He called it out to the cook and Andrew tried to get a read on the guy for about the hundredth time.

Andrew read ancient Greek, but he spoke a broken version of the modern language. Marco spoke broken English.

Andrew did not like the heavy feeling that the rules were not the same here, that he couldn't just go to a bar and flirt without having to watch his back.

Julia's death had ripped away the illusion of the island as peaceful in winter. Now everything felt a little ominous, a little too strange.

"Murder doesn't happen here," Marco said, reading the direction of Andrew's thoughts. His dark eyes dropped to the bar. "Not like in America."

"But you've got crime," Andrew said, trying not to sound defensive.

"How do you say . . . vandalismós? Or car thieves, but not murder. Not on Mykonos. Not often."

"Lucky me," Andrew said.

Marco gave him a confused cock of the head and went to get Andrew's food.

Chicken souvlaki with a side of dolmades. Andrew had been delighted to find the dolmades weren't the canned ones that showed up everywhere back home. They were good, but he couldn't pretend they were the reason he'd come.

He took a long sip of his wine. This was the good stuff, homemade, bottled here. He didn't think he'd ever be able to go back to American wine. Had the broken bottle had a label or had it been like the one Marco set on the bar?

Andrew connected to the taverna's Wi-Fi and looked up Julia's profile on the Berkeley site. He found the obituary for her son. Sam had drowned. It included a picture of Julia and her husband, Frank. The little boy had an infectious, golden smile, and a shock of black hair unlike either of his parents. Andrew frowned to think him gone so young.

"Julia?" Marco asked, startling Andrew as he peered over his shoulder.

Andrew hadn't seen him come out from behind the bar. Andrew caught his breath.

"I just don't know why anyone would kill her," he said.

"It's sad," Marco said.

"It is," Andrew agreed, closing the picture of the happy family. "The police said there are thieves on the island."

"Maybe she knew them," Marco said. "She was like you, a professor?"

"An archaeologist, yes. But I don't teach. Wait, are you saying she was helping them?"

Edward had dismissed it so quickly, but Julia's dig had been on the Continent. She had no reason to come to Mykonos, not in the winter.

"Or they wanted her to," Marco said.

Andrew thought of Edward, living alone in his hotel room, the same way Andrew lived and shuddered.

"Let me walk you home tonight," Marco said.

"You don't have to do that."

"I'd like to."

But then you'll also know where I live, Andrew thought.

"Don't you have to work?" he asked.

"For a while, but I can go early tonight."

Marco waved to indicate the empty bar.

Had he walked Julia home? Had he slipped behind her, or had they argued?

You only get one life, Andrew's father had liked to say.

And you only get one death, Andrew thought now.

He'd come here to see Marco, hadn't he?

"Okay," Andrew said. "I'll work until you're ready."

Marco grinned.

Andrew ate slowly as other hits from his parents' youth played over the speakers. The old men moved indoors, bringing the smell of smoke and the ocean with them. They eyed Andrew and he nodded before staring at his plate.

They seemed friendly enough, though Andrew didn't make eye contact. This wasn't that kind of bar.

He imagined Julia turning one of them down, imagined him following her home, wine bottle in hand.

Andrew opened his bag, took out his journal and a pen.

"What's that?" Marco asked. He made a show of wiping the bar with a towel, though Andrew couldn't see any reason, other than to stay nearby.

"My journal," Andrew said. "My dad gave it to me."

Italian leather, coffee- and travel-stained, Andrew had filled it with all of his notes, all of the sites he longed to excavate. They were mostly just dreams.

Archaeology was hard, slow work, endless sifting of dirt and brushing in the elusive search for how the common people had lived, the kind of people who didn't leave steles and monuments, the kind of people who didn't leave gold behind.

They were who Andrew wanted to find, their stories the past he wanted to recover.

"It's work mostly," he explained as Marco leaned closer. "All the sites and places I want to dig."

He flipped to the inscriptions he'd been struggling with.

The opposite page had his sketch of the grave. He'd drawn a death mask, like the kind found in Mycenae, though he had no idea if that was what the grave concealed.

Marco extended a finger to playfully tug the journal across the bar. He flipped through the pages and nodded.

"You like your work?" he asked, pushing the book back.

"I love it," Andrew confessed. "It's all I ever wanted to do, to be. What about you?"

"I do this for now," Marco said, waving a hand at the bar. "It would take money to be more."

"Is that what you want?"

Andrew couldn't tell if he was asking about Marco's job or something else. The language barrier was costing him context. Or maybe not. Marco smiled.

"Sometimes," he said.

Andrew warmed and did not know what to say.

Feeling like he'd pried, he went back to work.

A long while passed before Marco announced, "Okay. We can go."

He said something in rapid Greek to the cook and pulled on a leather jacket.

Andrew paid and tipped a little, enough to be generous but not look desperate, and stretched as he stood.

Marco opened the door for him.

He smelled a bit like the bar as Andrew passed, of the smoke, the food, and something else, a cologne like sandalwood and burnt oranges.

The outside air quickly scrubbed it away. Below, the ocean roiled, so black it was nearly invisible.

"It's later than I'd thought," Andrew said with a yawn.

"Yeah," Marco agreed.

He matched his stride to Andrew's and walked near enough that their shoulders almost brushed.

It could mean nothing. Greek men were more open with their affection than most Americans.

Andrew led Marco through the streets, back toward the hotel. He watched the alleys, spying for shadows and movement. He avoided the little square. At least he tried to. Mykonos Town, Chora, had been designed to confuse invading pirates. It worked just as well on visiting archaeologists.

"Are you from Mykonos?" Andrew asked.

"Patras, on the mainland. Have you been there?"

Andrew shook his head. He knew it was Greece's third-largest city, and a busy port, but hadn't visited.

Marco started humming the song from the tavern.

Michael Jackson. For all their xenomania, their obsession with foreign styles and trends, the Greeks could be strangely, cutely, stuck in the past.

"I've been to America," Marco volunteered.

"Where?"

"We went to San Francisco," Marco said. "I kept wondering who the murderers would be."

"It's not *that* bad," Andrew said.

"We watch a lot of your TV," Marco confessed.

"Who did you go with?" Andrew asked.

"My girlfriend," Marco said, edging closer.

"Ah," Andrew said, his steps suddenly heavier. "Are you still with her?"

"No," Marco said. "No more girlfriends."

"Never?"

"No," Marco said, reaching for Andrew's hand. "It's not my nature."

They exchanged a smile and Andrew let Marco hold his hand.

"This is me," he said when they reached the Electra, a three-story building that would do for now. Andrew would find a cheaper place when the rates went up.

Marco let go of Andrew and put his hands in his jean pockets, as if making an effort to keep them to himself.

"Will you come to the taverna tomorrow?" he asked, looking almost bashful.

"Maybe," Andrew said, smiling, already knowing he would.

"Okay."

Smiling, hands still in his pockets, Marco walked away.

The owner had left the front door cracked for him. That was how much they didn't worry, even with a fresh murder on the island.

Andrew climbed the stairs to his room and let himself inside. The taste of smoke still clung to the back of his throat.

He made certain the sliding glass door to the little balcony was closed and locked.

He checked the bathroom and the closet, just in case.

Though a bit grimy from the day, he'd shower in the morning, when there was a better chance for some hot water. That was one thing he missed about America, the chance to take a longer shower. The hotel's water was solar heated. At this hour it would make him shiver.

———

Edward didn't join him at the ferry. He was likely spending the day wrangling his latest batch of grad students by email or video call.

The digging was hard, but Andrew didn't mind. He liked having the site to himself.

It was near the temple of Athena, close to the island's highest point. He could see the ocean from here, could almost pretend that he had Delos all to himself.

Despite the sparse landscape, it was easy to imagine the glory days of the Delian League, when Athens ruled the seas.

Andrew had brought plenty of water and a few sandwiches. He lost himself in the work, digging and sifting, scratching notes, and cataloging what little he found.

Today might be the day he broke through to the grave. In a way he wanted to savor it, to make it last. This would be his first big find and, with it, he'd truly start his career, the life he'd built for himself and wanted to live.

Standing in the pit, he realized the sun was close to setting.

He did not know if the last boat would wait for him or how thorough they'd be about counting heads.

Andrew hurried to grab his bag and notes, but he could not leave the grave open.

He scrambled to place the tarp and stones to weigh it down, knowing it was likely already too late. He hurried down the hill, toward the dock, but it was getting dark. He had to go carefully or risk his footing. This wasn't anywhere he wanted to break an ankle. It wasn't like he had cell service here.

He passed the ruins.

He'd try the ferry office. If no one answered his knock, he'd head to the museum. Maybe he'd get lucky enough to find an overnight guard, or maybe there was Wi-Fi and he could call someone. He would not panic.

After all, there was nothing to fear here. The island was mostly abandoned, mostly, which he remembered when a pale cat crossed his path, startling him into making a noise that he was relieved no one was around to hear.

A boat stood at the dock. Andrew exhaled and started forward until he spied a man coming toward him. Twilight made a shadow of him, but he walked with purpose.

Andrew cast about but there was nowhere to hide, nowhere to run.

The man waved and came closer.

"Andrew?" Marco called.

"What are you doing here?" Andrew asked, letting out a long breath.

"You missed the ferry, so I asked Spiros to bring me." Marco pointed toward the boat.

"Thank you," Andrew said. "I was worried I was going to have to spend the night here."

Marco stepped forward and hugged him.

"This way," Marco said, smiling as he let Andrew go.

Andrew recognized Spiros as one of the old men from the tavern. He looked the part of a sailor, with a navy blue peacoat and a hat that framed the steely wool of his beard and cragged features.

He exchanged a polite *yassas* with Andrew and began the trip back to Mykonos as soon as Marco and Andrew had taken their seats.

Andrew had never made the crossing after dark. The boat's lights bounced across the choppy water. It was cold.

Spiros drove and chain smoked. The wind whipped the taste past Andrew's nose as he exchanged shy glances with Marco.

"How did you know I missed the ferry?"

"I had the night off and wanted to surprise you, but you weren't at the dock."

"I'm glad you came," Andrew said, warming as they locked eyes.

"You got caught up in your work, didn't you?" Marco asked, his eyes laughing.

"How did you know?"

"I've watched you. It's something you do."

"It is," Andrew confessed.

They docked and climbed out. Marco passed Spiros a wad of Euros. They spoke quickly in hurried Greek.

"Thank you," Andrew told the old man, who only grunted. Maybe Andrew could buy him a glass of ouzo next time he saw him.

Marco matched Andrew's pace as they headed toward the town.

"I can pay you back," Andrew said.

"You do not have to."

"At least let me buy you dinner?"

"All right, but not at the taverna."

Andrew laughed.

They found a place that was pricey for Andrew's budget, but the couple running it seemed glad for the business. Andrew might even have called it romantic.

The slow pace of the meal did not bother him. They ate. They talked. A few more words of Greek fell into place, and he felt pretty certain that he no longer misread the shine in Marco's eyes.

Andrew slammed the glass of ouzo they offered at the end. It wasn't to his taste, but it would be rude to decline.

Marco grew more animated as they walked away.

They did not hold hands, but they walked near enough to one another that their shoulders often brushed. Neither suggested it, but the charge to the air said they'd be keeping one another company back at the hotel.

They were in the little square before Andrew had registered the route he'd taken.

A man entered from the other direction.

He wasn't remarkable looking, with brown hair and an average build, but something like malice radiated off him.

Andrew froze when he recognized him. Frank had changed since his picture in the paper, since Sam had died.

He looked wild-eyed, more than a little crazed.

"Was it you?" he demanded.

His hand shook as lifted a gun and pointed it at Marco.

Andrew swallowed hard and froze. It felt like everything had stopped—his breathing, his heart.

"Was. It. You?" Frank repeated, punctuating each word with a jab of the gun in their direction.

"What are you talking about?" Andrew asked, raising his hands.

"Julia," Frank said with another jab of the barrel.

"No," Marco said. "I didn't kill anyone."

"Of course you didn't kill her." Frank stepped closer. He wouldn't miss at that range, no matter how hard he shook. He smelled sour and smoky, like he'd bathed in bourbon and tried to sleep it off in an alley. "Were you sleeping with her? Were you Sam's father?"

"No," Marco repeated, eyes darting between Frank and Andrew.

All the gold had drained out of his skin, and he looked more than a little confused.

"What is going on, Frank?" Andrew asked, trying to sound calm.

"I thought Sam was mine. Mine."

The gun waved back and forth, dancing between them.

Something clattered in one of the nearby alleys.

Andrew did not think. He knew that if he did, he wouldn't act. He leaped forward, swinging his bag at Frank's arm. It connected awkwardly.

The gun went off and Andrew found himself tackling Frank to the ground.

It wasn't anything like a fight on television. Andrew kicked and punched. Then Marco was there, trying to hold Frank's arm so he could not fire again. He did not know how long it went on, he and Marco trying to keep the larger man pinned.

At one point Andrew kneed Frank in the balls. He wasn't proud of it, but it bought him a heaving breath.

Then the police were there, rushing into the square.

Andrew was tossed aside. Frank was restrained and dragged into a sitting position.

Andrew and Marco took heaving breaths and exchanged a glance as the gun was collected and bagged.

"Are you okay?" Andrew asked.

Marco nodded. "You?"

"Yeah."

"Doctor Patras." It was the cop from the night he'd found Julia. "Are you all right?"

He didn't seem worried about Marco.

"We're fine," Andrew said.

"Who is he?" Marco asked.

"Julia's husband," Andrew said.

"He took a catamaran from the mainland," the cop explained.

"That was why you asked me about how I arrived," Andrew said.

"Yes. We'd thought he'd left the island."

"Why did he kill her?" Marco asked, sounding sad.

"He found out their child wasn't his," Andrew said.

The cop nodded.

"It is always the husband, though Professor Miller made some calls on our behalf. That was how we knew he'd left California."

"He came halfway around the world to murder her," Andrew said. "That's horrible."

They were already dragging Frank away. The man was sobbing. Andrew didn't know if it was grief, alcohol, or some combination of the two.

Despite everything, his heart twinged with a bit of ache.

He remembered his dad, the moments after, the long beep of the monitor, when Andrew had puked from grief.

Marco inched closer, though he stopped short of putting his arm around Andrew's shoulders.

Andrew understood. He did not know how the cops would take it.

"Do you need a statement or anything?" Andrew asked.

"Not tonight. Go home."

Andrew nodded.

"Let me walk you," Marco said.

Andrew had no interest in arguing, though the anticipation and the buzz of the ouzo had chilled to ice.

Still, Andrew did not say no when Marco invited himself inside. He did not protest when Marco kissed him.

———

A pounding on the door brought Andrew into the daylight, bringing him back from a golden, happy dream. He lay alone, naked.

"Andrew!" Edward called from the other side of the door. "Are you in there?"

"A minute!" Andrew called.

He scrambled into his clothes and opened the door to find a harried-looking Edward standing on the other side. Sweat beaded his bald head. He'd been running.

"Are you all right?" he asked. "I just heard the news."

"Yeah. Sorry. I didn't sleep well." He hoped he didn't blush as he said it. "You didn't have to wait for me."

"Any damage?" Edward asked.

"No," Andrew said. "Julia's husband attacked us, but they got him. The cops said he wasn't the father. That's why he killed her."

Edward hung his head low.

"Julia left him in America to raise the boy while she pursued her career."

"It was more than that," Andrew said. "He wanted to know if Marco was the father. That's why he stayed on the island after he killed her."

Edward shook his head.

Andrew tried not to let his eyes fix on the empty bed.

"Let me get my shoes on and we can go," he said.

"Are you sure? You can take the day off. You had a hell of a night."

Andrew reached for his boots to hide his blush.

"I'm sure," he said. "Let's just find some coffee before we head over."

He lifted his bag and found it lighter than it should be.

"Where is it?" he asked, riffling through the contents.

"What?"

"My notebook."

They scanned the room, but there was no place for it to hide. Had it fallen out during his fight with Frank? No, the bag had been latched, and the weight had felt right when they'd walked back to the hotel.

Something cold slid into Andrew's guts.

"We need to go check on the site," he said.

"What?" Edward asked. "Why?"

"Marco," Andrew said.

They hurried to the docks, Edward got winded early, and Andrew forced himself to slow down, to let Edward keep up. They caught the next ferry, and Andrew drummed his fingers on the metal rail the entire time.

They raced off the dock, marched up the hill.

Andrew's stomach sank and sank as they climbed. He raced ahead, leaving Edward to catch up.

He found what he knew he would find.

The tarp had been pulled aside. It fluttered like a sail, rippling, weighed down by one of the rocks.

Dirt lay everywhere, rudely piled, the final layers were broken and all of Andrew's careful work destroyed.

There were bits, debris that he might sort through to learn something, but the grave lay empty, the contents ransacked.

Whatever had been there, whatever the mystery and the final prize, had been looted.

"Andrew . . ." Edward said, catching up. He froze, turned red with rage.

"We'll go back," Edward said. "We'll get him."

"You know as well as I do that he's already gone," Andrew said with a shake of his head.

It had never felt so heavy.

"I don't understand," Edward said. "Why would he do this?"

"He wanted to be more," Andrew heard himself say as if from somewhere far away. "And he needed money to do it."

"This is a disaster. The university will blame you. The Ministry of Culture could pull our permission to dig." Edward lifted his clenched fingers. No doubt he would have pulled at his hair if he'd had any. "How could this happen?"

"Human nature," Andrew muttered, the notes of the song echoing in his memory.

The golden memory of the night before remained warm and dreamlike. How could that be? He couldn't reconcile it, that feeling, to this. Edward was right. It was a disaster.

You only get one life, Andrew thought.

He'd built his so carefully. Now he had the terrible sense that it was over.

You only get one death.

RICK BLEIWEISS

PRETTY YOUNG THING

MORNING

After killing Louise, the hitwoman from the mainland who had been sent to Maui to take *him* out, Walker, New York's top hitman who was hiding out at the Surfland Resort in Kihei, wheeled the accessories cart she had left outside his door and rummaged through it until he found what he was looking for: an empty jumbo, heavy-gauge garbage bag. He placed his hands under her ample chest to lift her lifeless blood-soaked body into the bag, and thought, *what a shame, you were one looker, dar-ling.* Once she was fully crammed into the trash bag, he tied it closed, dragged it to the bedroom closet, and then went back to the cart.

He used the bleach, soap, rags, and paper towels to clean up the blood that had splattered on the walls and floor when his bullet exploded into her head. Once Walker had scrubbed the area as spotless as those cleaning agents would allow, he took a kitchen knife and dislodged the bullet she had shot at him from the wall it was embedded in. Then he placed all the towels and rags and the projectile in a smaller garbage bag and threw it into the bedroom closet as well.

Walker circled around the bed to the bathroom, washed his hands, and then went to the front door. He pushed the cart out of the condo and into the elevator. When it got to the ground floor, he wheeled the cart through the parking lot into the dumpster enclosure and placed it next to the garbage bin sitting inside. Then he went back to the condo to retrieve the garbage bags in the closet. They were a struggle even for a man of his strength, but Walker was able to carry and drag them into the elevator and eventually throw them into the dumpster, perspiring the whole time from the oppressively hot midday sun.

When he closed the doors to the garbage shed, Walker wiped the dripping sweat off his face with the bottom of his shirt and looked at the two buildings the parking lot serviced. After scanning all the balconies, he was confident that no one had seen him throwing out what would look like heavy garbage.

Once he was back in the condo, Walker changed into a new shirt, and inhaled five deep, cleansing, relaxing breaths before walking to the couch in the living room. From his Marine training and years of success as a hitman, the belief that he could deal with anything that came his way was ingrained into him, so he calmly sat down and phoned his friend Junior Hanks.

Junior answered the call on the second ring.

"Hey, Junior, how goes it? Where are you?"

"Home, Walker, doin' nothin'. It's been pourin' puppies and kittens here all day. Manhattan's so wet I'd have to wear a bathing suit and flip-flops if I went out. My old man would never have tried a hit in this weather, he'd have been afraid it would've rusted his piece. And like him, I prefer staying nice and dry in my apartment. What about you? You still in Hawaii? You okay?"

Walker shifted on the couch. "Yep. It's been hotter than Hades— even though it rained last night it didn't make a difference. But all is just dandy. You know that hitman they sent after me? Surprise of all surprises, it wasn't a hitman, it was a hitwoman. Her name was Louise, not Lou."

Junior *was* surprised. "No kiddin'? I guess if you're talkin' to me, she didn't get you."

"It was close," Walker reported, "but I nailed her just before she got a chance to put a slug in my head. There was a lot of blood, Junior, more than usual 'cause we were right next to each other. I cleaned it all up pretty decent, but just as soon as we hang up, I'm gonna find a new place to stay. I paid for another week here, so they won't be checking on this condo for another few days. I'm gonna make myself invisible for a while."

"Speaking of invisible, what'd you do with Louise?"

"She's in a garbage bag in a dumpster outside. You think New York's got a lot of dumpsters, Junior? It looks like they got more per square foot here, and that made it an easy throw down."

Junior doubted that. "C'mon, Walker. That ain't possible. There's a dumpster here for every building. Sometimes two or three, or more."

Walker inwardly smiled. "You got me. I was exaggerating a bit. But you get the idea. You know what else? That Louise had a nifty little plastic gun and some bullets. I saved it before I tossed her. It fits right into my sock without makin' too big a bulge, and that's where it's stashed right now."

Junior was intrigued. "A plastic gun? And it works?"

"Sure does. It almost got me. If I was a bettin' man, I'd wager somebody made it with one of those 3D printers."

"Hey, maybe I should get one. I guess you can use them to make a lot more than I thought."

Walker responded, "Probably can. When I go out, I'll be puttin' my regular piece in my waistband as usual, but with this little popgun in my sock, I'll feel extra safe."

"Cool."

"She also had a phony US Marshal badge and identification card. I'm gonna doctor that up, and then I'm goin' out to find one of those tourist photo machines and do the same to the driver's license I traded for a couple of days ago. That way I'll have two IDs that say I'm Fred Harding."

"Think they'll send someone else after you from here?"

"No idea. If you hear anything you know how to reach me. But with a new name, it'll take them an awful long time to find me even if they do send someone. Listen, mostly, I just called to let you know I'm okay and tell you that the hit man was a broad. I'm headin' out now to rent another condo. I'll call you again after I'm settled in."

Walker ended the call, positioned his gun so that it felt comfortable, and draped his shirt over it, so no bulge was visible. Then he donned his sunglasses and a cap with an embroidered pineapple on the crown and left the apartment. He found a photo machine two blocks away, had his picture taken—without the cap on—and walked away with a strip of three passport-sized photos. Then he purchased a package of laminating paper and other supplies he'd need to forge the two IDs.

On his way back to Surfland, Walker passed the Oceanside Resort, a large building with a sign at its entrance: Units for Rent. He went in and took the only apartment they had available, a two-bedroom condo with a full ocean view, registering as Fred Harding.

Once he moved all his belongings into the Oceanside, Walker set about converting the IDs. He was diligent in making the two pieces of identification look real, and despite Fred's license being old-style with no holograms or fancy watermarks it still took him a few hours to get them done. By the time he had completed both it had already become evening, so he called Junior again before it got too late back East.

"Where are you now?" Junior asked.

"I'm in the new condo watching the Pacific Ocean reflect the moon. You should come here sometime; you'd like it. I've got a two bedroom so if you wanna come now I can put you up. I am getting hungry though, so I'm gonna go out and grab some food when we hang up. There are some decent kitchens around here."

Junior laughed, "What do you know about good food? You're like a human billy goat, man, you eat anything."

Walker laughed back. "Can't argue with that, Junior. But I gotta keep my figure, and this place has some tasty things I've never had before. You ever had mahi-mahi tacos?"

Junior responded, "Can't say that I have. But personally, they sound disgusting."

Walker disagreed. "They're not. Your loss."

Walker looked at the time on his cell phone. "Hey, gotta get going before everything's closed. Places don't stay open late like in New York. I'll ring you again soon. Maybe tomorrow."

When the call ended, Walker once again stashed the gun in his waistband and made sure his shirt covered it. He put a wad of bills and the doctored driver's license in one front pocket of his slacks and the Marshal ID in the other. Last, he put on his cap. Even though it was relatively dark outside he had gotten used to wearing it and enjoyed the feel of it on his head. Then he went out to get some dinner.

After he ate two servings of fish tacos at Coconuts, he paid the bill and walked down the stairs to their nearly deserted parking lot. Just as he turned to go toward his apartment, a girl ran into him, thudded against his body, and started pounding on his chest with ineffectual fists, crying out, "Don't kill me! Please! I don't wanna die!"

EARLIER THAT EVENING A FEW STREETS AWAY

Sarah Franklin stayed so busy doing her homework, texting with her friends, and then checking out their suggestions of a few YouTube channels she hadn't visited before, that she never changed from her red shorts and pink halter into her pajamas. Looking up from her phone, Sarah's gaze went to her bedroom window, and she was delighted when she saw that it was dark enough outside to use the telescope that she had asked her parents to get for her sixteenth birthday. She had been disappointed that she couldn't use it the night before, on her birthday, because rain and clouds filled the sky and made viewing impossible. But on this clear evening whose crescent moon wasn't bright enough to affect her view, Sarah was eagerly anticipating being able to see Jupiter and Saturn's rings.

She put her phone down on her nightstand, noticing the digital display change to exactly 9:50 p.m. Then she walked to the window, raised it so that it was fully open, and moved the telescope so that it protruded out of the window and pointed toward the heavens.

As she looked out the window, she noticed the naked bathroom light in their next-door neighbor's house was shining brightly. Since the bathroom window was directly across from her bedroom with only a small side yard between the houses separating the two rooms, Sarah hoped that either Dave or Doris would turn it off so it wouldn't interfere with her viewing.

From Sarah's vantage point she also had a view of Dave and Doris's front door, and she was glad that the light over it wasn't also on.

Unfortunately, it didn't remain off for long. Sarah saw a dark sedan drive up and park in front of Dave and Doris's house. Then three men got out of the car and walked to their front door. One of the men started loudly rapping on the door, and as he did the light above the entrance came on.

Darn, Sarah thought, *that's going to make it even harder to see the two planets.*

When neither Dave nor Doris appeared at the door, the man began banging on it more forcefully, while one of the other men shouted, "Let us in or we're gonna knock this door down."

Sarah was starting to get concerned, and a bit scared, but she was transfixed by what was happening. And then a rapid series of events unfolded in Dave and Doris's house that Sarah witnessed from her window.

The third man, who Sarah could see well enough to determine that he was a large, burly guy, moved in front of the other two and put his shoulder against the door. He leaned into it and when he pushed on the door it gave way, separating from the doorjamb, and cracked open. Once it did, Sarah saw the three men go into the house.

Just after that, Sarah saw Doris enter the bathroom across from her and throw something into the toilet, but before she could flush it, one of the men appeared at the door. He grabbed the back of Doris's robe and roughly pulled her out of the bathroom, while another of the men went into the room and took whatever Doris had thrown into the toilet out of it. Sarah saw that he was holding a gun in his left hand.

Just before he exited, he looked out the window and stared across the yard.

A chill ran up Sarah's spine as she realized he had probably seen her watching him. *Shit, shit,* she thought as she ran to the light switch on her bedroom wall, hoping it wasn't too late for her room to be dark. Then she crouched down and crept back to the window and peered out over the bottom sill.

She didn't see anything else but began to hear a lot of loud shouting coming from inside the house and then what sounded like a car back-fire, or a gunshot, followed by a piercing scream.

Sarah backed away from the window and ran to her parents' bed-room.

Sarah had no idea that at that exact moment, as the digital clock on her father's nightstand flashed 10:00 p.m., her mother, Jean Frank-lin, removed her panties, the last piece of the clothing she had been wearing, and eased into bed with Sarah's father, Bob. They were both anticipating a passionate session of affection as they started to embrace and caress each other in the master bedroom of their ranch-style home on the southern end of Kihei in Maui. With the unseasonably torrid heat of the October day gone, their unclothed bodies were touched by a soft, warm breeze blowing through their open bedroom window from the Pacific Ocean a block away.

Before they could become truly intimate, an insistent rapping on their bedroom door diverted their attention from each other, and then they heard Sarah cry out, "Mom. Dad. I have to come in!"

"Honey, we're busy. Can't it wait?" Jean responded.

Sarah urgently pleaded through the door, "No, it can't wait. Please can I come in? It's important. Really important."

Realizing that no matter what Sarah wanted, the intimacy he was about to enjoy with his wife was probably gone, Bob said, "All right. Give us a second."

"Hurry!" Sarah implored them.

Her parents hastily picked up the clothes they had discarded on the floor beside their bed and put them back on their cooling bodies. Once they were mostly dressed, Bob strode to the door. When he opened it, Sarah ran into the room and sat down on the edge of the bed. She seemed visibly upset—trembling and shaking to her mother's eye. "What's wrong honey? What's happened that's so important?"

"I was looking out my window and I saw something next door." Sarah exclaimed nervously.

"At Doris and Dave's house?" Bob asked.

"Yes," Sarah replied with a sound of urgency.

"What'd you see?"

Sarah quickly recounted what she had seen and heard in the greatest detail she could remember.

Thinking for just a moment about what their daughter had said, Bob asked Sarah, "Are you sure this is what you saw and heard? You have a very good imagination, baby. This sounds more like a TV show than something that would happen next door to us."

Sarah insisted, "Dad, believe me. I'm sure. It happened. Just like I told you and Mom."

Jean stood up and put her slippers on. "Bob, this doesn't sound good. Don't you think we should call 911?"

Bob replied, "I'm not certain the situation is as dire as Sarah is reporting it to be. Why don't we check on Doris and Dave first?"

"Don't go there!" Sarah pleaded.

Bob reached for the cell phone next to the clock on his nightstand. "Let's give them a call and see if Dave or Doris answers. I'm hoping it's nothing, but we should check to make sure. We shouldn't be sending the police on a wild goose chase if it's not as bad as Sarah thinks it is."

The phone rang once. Twice. Three times. Four times. On the fifth ring a man's voice answered, tentatively saying, "Hello?"

Bob asked, "Dave, is that you?"

"Who's this?"

"It's Bob. Next door."

Dave anxiously said, "Bob, I can't talk now."

"Dave, is everything all right there?"

Dave unconvincingly said, "Uh, yes."

Jean leaned into the phone as Bob turned it toward her. "Dave, are you sure? Is Doris okay?"

Bob whispered to Jean, "Tell him Sarah thought she heard screams."

Jean nodded that she would. "Dave, did you or Doris scream? Sarah said it sounded like there was screaming coming from your house."

Dave responded, "Jean, I— I— I don't know what you're talking about. I have to go." And then the line went dead.

Bob and Jean looked at each other in concern and confusion.

Jean took the phone from Bob. "I'm calling 911."

Before she could even press the 9 a loud banging started resounding through their house, coming from their front door. Then they heard a man's voice shouting through the door, "Let us in or we'll break this damn door down."

Bob quickly turned to Sarah. "Do you see the men's faces, baby?"

Sarah started shaking, "I did, Dad."

Jean added, "And you think they saw you?"

"I think so. One of the men looked right at my window when he was in the bathroom. I don't know if he saw me or not, but he might've 'cause my light was on."

Jean continued dialing 911, but before the call was connected the front door burst open. Two large men holding guns pushed into the house and one of them called out, "Sarah, where are you, sweetie?"

Then the other shouted, "Bob and Jean. Where are you?"

Jean began hurriedly describing what was happening to the 911 operator, while Bob reached under the bed and pulled out his gun case. In his haste to open it he fumbled with the lock losing precious seconds in the process.

While he was unlatching the case, he told Sarah, "We'll be fine. Daddy will take care of this. You go out the back door and wait by the pool for us. We'll come and get you when it's over. Go, now!"

Sarah started crying. "I don't want to leave you."

Jean stopped talking to the operator and sternly commanded Sarah, "Listen to your father. Go out back and wait for us."

Sarah reluctantly tiptoed out of the bedroom and dashed out the back door.

Bob got the case unlocked and took out his Glock, muttering, "I wish this was an AR-15. It would be much more effective against multiple intruders."

As Sarah stood and shook by the pool, she saw all the lights in the house go out, and then five flashes briefly illuminate the inside along with loud sounds, similar to what she heard coming from Dave and Doris's house. She started toward the door but froze when it opened, and her mother staggered out of it with a growing circle of red spreading through her clothes in the area of her abdomen. Jean gasped, "Run, Sarah, run!" as she fell forward.

Sarah started toward her, but Jean screamed again, "Run! Now!"

Sarah heard footsteps inside the house approaching the back door, and in that instant, she started dashing to the backyard gate, tears flowing freely and her body convulsing in fright.

She got through the gate and ran as fast as she could away from the house but kept looking back to see if any of the men were after her. Just before she turned the first corner toward the ocean, she saw one of the men running through the gate in her direction.

Sarah ran as fast as her legs would take her, heading toward South Kihei Road, where she hoped a policeman would be present.

The man behind her wasn't gaining on Sarah, but he wasn't falling further back either and when she reached the main thoroughfare, he was still a block behind her.

She ran into the largely empty parking lot of a strip shopping center, most of whose stores were closed, and momentarily stopped. She looked around to see if there were any police nearby, and when she saw none, she turned to start running again. But she hadn't noticed that another man was walking toward her, and she ran right into him.

Her first instinct was to lash out, and she started harmlessly pounding her fists on his steel-hard body. "Don't kill me. Please. I don't wanna die."

The man grabbed her shoulders to steady her. "Hold on, kid. I'm not gonna hurt you. You in trouble?"

Sarah looked up at the man who was towering three-quarters-of-a-foot over her, and then pointed at the man with the gun rushing across the lot toward them. "I—I think he shot my mom and dad."

Before she could say or do anything else, the stranger grabbed her arm and started dragging her toward the back of the parking lot behind the stores. Once they reached that more secluded area, he told her, "I'll help you. Get behind that trash bin and stay down."

Still shaking and sobbing, Sarah ran to the dumpster and crouched behind it.

When the chaser with the gun appeared at the edge of the building he was gasping for breath. He looked at Walker and managed to blurt out, "Man, I'm not in shape for this." Then he scanned the area and asked, "Where is she?"

"What d'ya want with her?" Walker calmly asked.

"Listen, you, funny man in the pineapple cap, it's none of your business."

"I've made it my business."

The gunman replied, "Then I'm gonna kill you both, asshole."

Before he could say another word or raise his gun, Walker reached behind his back and in a lightning-fast move pulled out his gun from the waistband of his pants and shot the gunman through his left eye, killing him instantly.

When the shot rang out, Sarah screamed and didn't stop screaming until Walker came over to her, picked her up from the ground, hugged her quivering body to his, and said, "Ssh. It's gonna be okay. That guy's not gonna hurt you. Not now, not ever."

After a few seconds, Sarah pulled away from Walker. Still sobbing, she shrieked, "You killed him!"

"I did," he replied, "to stop him from killing both of us."

"But you killed him!"

"I did. It was either him that was going to be dead or you and me, and I chose him."

"There were two others at my house. What about them? And, oh my God! What about my parents?" Then Sarah's wobbly legs couldn't hold her up no longer and she collapsed to the ground.

Walker crouched down next to her. "What's your name?"

"Sarah. Sarah Franklin."

"Listen to me, Sarah Franklin, nothing is going to happen to you now that you're with me. You take us to your home and let's find out how your parents are."

From his years as a hitman, Walker knew how killers worked, and he expected that they'd find her parents were dead. But he lied to Sarah to calm her. "I'll bet they're okay and worried sick about you."

"You think so?"

"Let's go find out. A pretty young thing like you shouldn't have to worry about her safety, or her parents'. You can tell me what happened on the way to your house. How far is it?"

"Only a few streets," Sarah replied. Gaining back some of her composure and strength, Sarah stood up and said, "I'll show you. What's your name?"

As Walker rose from his crouch, he put the warm gun back in his waistband and quickly thought about how he wanted to answer her. He realized he wanted to say something comforting to her, so he said, "My name is Fred Harding, but my friends call me Walker, and with what we just went through, I think you now qualify as a friend. What d'ya say, Sarah?"

Sarah turned her head up toward him. "Why are you called Walker if your name's Fred Harding?"

Walker took her by the arm and guided her away from the trash bin. "It's a complicated story. Maybe I'll tell you sometime, but we need to get away from here right now.

Walker went over to the gunman, picked his gun off the ground, and put it next to his own in his pants waistband. He lifted up the body and tossed it into the dumpster, covering it with papers and trash. Then he and Sarah set out to walk the few blocks to her house.

On their way, Sarah, still shaking, thanked Walker. "I don't know what would've happened to me if you weren't there. Do you really think my parents are okay?"

Walker lied again, "I think so."

Sarah turned to him, "But I saw Mom bleeding and she was hurt."

"Doesn't mean she's dead, kiddo. What's her name?"

Sarah told him, "Jean. And my dad's Bob." Then she said, "You don't sound like you're from around here."

"I'm not," Walker confirmed. "I'm from the mainland. But I'm considering living here. I just ended something with a woman who followed me here, and I'm thinkin' I might like it better on Maui than anywhere else right about now."

"How come you carry a gun? Are you an undercover cop?"

Walker thought about how he was going to answer that question and then said, "Nope. Not a cop. I'm kind of like a private cop. I get hired to go after bad people and make sure they don't hurt good people."

Sarah liked that. "So, you're kind of a guardian. Like you're protecting me now."

That struck a positive chord with Walker. "Yeah. Sort of like that. In fact, I like that a lot—that I'm a guardian and a protector. That's how I felt in the Marines—like I was protecting people. Thanks, kid, you've given me a new way to look at myself."

Sarah moved herself a little closer to Walker as they walked. "I like having a protector. You're like my white knight. It makes me feel safer."

Surprised at how much he enjoyed hearing her say that Walker took off his pineapple cap and put it on Sarah. "That'll protect your head and remind you that I'm protecting the rest of you."

Sarah tugged the brim down so that the cap was sitting more securely over her hair and ran her fingers across the pineapple. "Thanks. Can I ask you a question?"

"Sure. What d'ya want to know?"

"Do you really think I'm pretty? You called me that before."

Walker smiled. "I do, kid. How old are you?"

Sarah replied, "Sixteen. Yesterday was my birthday."

"Well, happy birthday, Sarah Franklin. Let me tell you, if I was twenty years younger and you were twenty years older, I'd make a play for you. But I'm not, and you're not, and that's the end of that. But yes, you are pretty, birthday girl."

Sarah glowed inside and momentarily forgot about the potential horror awaiting them when they reached her house. But her reverie quickly ended. "Walker, what about the other two guys? The man you shot wasn't the one who I think saw me. What if they're still at my house?" Sarah began to shake slightly again.

Walker put his arm around her and stopped their walking. "Listen to me, Sarah—as long as I'm with you, nothing is going to happen to you. I took care of that guy and I'll take care of the other two. Nobody's gonna harm you while I'm around. Got it?"

Sarah wanted to believe Walker. "Yeah. I hope you're right."

"I am," he said confidently. "Now let's get to your house and see how your parents are."

When Sarah and Walker turned the corner of the block that led to her house they stopped. Before them a beehive of activity was taking place— six police cars with steadily flashing lights were parked at random angles in front of both Sarah's house and the house next door. Sitting among them were two ambulances whose rear doors were open showing what appeared to be paramedics arranging supplies and making preparations of some sort. Numerous police personnel and medics were continuously walking, and sometimes running, in and out of both brightly lit houses, which looked to have every light in each house turned on.

Sarah and Walker could faintly hear unintelligible conversations taking place between the various police personnel there, whoever they were speaking with on their radios and handsets, and the paramedics.

Walker had witnessed many similar scenes in New York after his hits so he understood that the events taking place were most likely the results of a major tragedy and deaths. He thought, but didn't say aloud, *that's not good.*

"I don't see Mom and Dad," Sarah reported as her eyes began to tear up, "where are they?" She started running toward the house but only got three or four steps before Walker grabbed her arm and stopped her. "Hold on, Sarah. Those other two guys could be lurking around waitin' to see if you return. I don't want to give them a clear shot at you between here and the house."

Sarah looked at Walker with tears streaming down her cheeks. "You think they can do that even with all the police there?"

"I do," he firmly replied. "None of the cops are in their vehicles so the bad guys could be sittin' near here in their car. It'd be easy for them to shoot you, and then drive away before the cops knew what happened."

"But I wanna see my parents."

"I know, kid, just trust me a little, and we'll find out how they are, really quickly. Just not by bargin' in over there."

"Okay. But what're we gonna do?"

Walker began formulating a plan. He wanted to guard against Sarah being hurt, but also didn't want to come into much contact with the cops, since he had three guns on him, his piece, the one from the shooter who was chasing Sarah, and the plastic gun in his sock.

"Here's what we're gonna do," he told her, "You see that row of thick hedges next to that house across the street? We'll walk over there together and you're gonna get behind them and sit on the ground so no one can see you from the road. I'm gonna give you that shooter's gun so I don't have it on me. Will you do that?"

Sarah started to get scared again. "No, don't leave me, I won't feel safe if I'm not with you."

Walker looked her directly in her eyes. "Did I tell you nothin' will happen to you? That I'd keep you safe?"

She softly answered, "Yes."

"Then you have to believe me and trust me. That'll be the safest place for you while I go check out what's happenin' and find out how your parents are."

"But I'm scared."

"I know you are, kid. I would be too, if it was me. But we both gotta do what I'm suggestin'. It's the only way to keep you safe and for me to find out what happened to your folks. Just stay behind the bushes until I get back."

They crossed the street, Sarah sat down behind the hedge and Walker handed her the shooter's gun. "You ever held one of these?"

Gripping the weapon with both hands, Sarah answered, "No. Never."

"In that case, put it on the ground next to you and leave it there until I come back."

Sarah placed the gun on the grass as Walker left for her house.

When Walker got there, a policeman stopped him just before he reached the back of the ambulances. "This is a crime scene. Please turn around and leave. You can stand with all those other gawkers." He pointed to a group of people milling around across the street behind a police barrier who were watching everything that was going on.

Walker reached into his pants pocket and took out the Marshal badge and ID card. The officer looked at it and handed it back to Walker. "So how can I help you, Marshal? You got some interest in this?"

"Nope," Walker answered, "I happened to be in the neighborhood, saw the activity, and thought I'd see if I could be of some assistance. I'm tracking down an escaped felon from back East, and you never know where he could have run to or what he might be involved in."

The officer pointed to the two houses. "You're guy a murderer?"

Walker answered, "Nope. Drugs."

The officer moved in closer to Walker. He pointed to the house next to Sarah's. "We think this was a drug deal gone bad in that one, and the people in this one"—he indicated Sarah's home—"were innocent victims. We're pretty sure it's a group of locals who did this, not some out-of-towners—we've been watching that house for a while, but unfortunately, we didn't have any eyes on it tonight. We think one of the gangs—a remnant of the Company—were responsible, and they're some bad, bad people. Left no witnesses, as usual."

Walker leaned against one of the ambulances. "How many?"

The officer replied, "Four. Two in each house. The guy in this one had a Glock, but he was no match for whoever did this. If it was done by the Triad or Yakuza gangs, he had no chance. Zero."

Walker responded, "I didn't know you had gangs out here in the middle of the ocean."

"We do," the officer affirmed. "Most of it started on Oahu but it's spread out to all the islands. Where you from? You sound like New York."

Walker didn't want there to be any current connection to New York and remembered that Fred Harding's license was from Illinois. "You got me. Born in New York but moved to Chi-town."

The officer shuffled his feet, "Never been to either. One of our guys went to Chicago last year. Said it felt as cold as the North Pole when he was down by the lake. That's not for me."

Walker hoped the officer wouldn't ask more questions about Chicago, and he didn't. "Well, either way, you got your gangs and we got ours. Same MO, different names."

Walker nodded in understanding.

The cop went on, "We think the ones in this house had a daughter, but lucky for her she wasn't home. If she was, she'd be on one of those carts like her parents. At least I hope she wasn't there. If she was and saw them and ran, they'll track her down and do to her what they did to her parents. We're going to have to locate her before they do. Let me tell you, I'd hate to be the one to have to break this news to her if she wasn't there when this happened."

Walker got a knot in the pit of his stomach thinking how he was going to have to tell Sarah, and what he was going to say to her. He realized he should get back to her quickly. "Doesn't seem like much I can do. Thanks for the info. Terrible thing, though."

"It sure is. We don't have many like this on the island. It's one of the worst I've ever seen." The officer's hand radio squawked, and he excused himself. He went into Sarah's house just as paramedics came out of the front door wheeling two body bags on gurneys which they brought to the ambulances.

Walker turned away and headed back to Sarah. As he walked the short block to where she was hidden, he tried to figure out what he was going to say to her. When he didn't come up with an answer, Walker did firm up a resolution that even if it put his life in danger, he wasn't going to let the gangs, or anyone else, harm her. Walker thought, *it really is a strange sensation safeguarding someone rather than taking them out, but I kind of enjoy feeling that way. It reminds me of my time in the Marines.*

When he got to Sarah, Walker still didn't know what he was going to say to her or how he was going to tell her that both her parents were dead.

NEW YORK

Back in New York, Al "Smokey" Challow was still waiting for Louise's call telling him that Walker was dead.

He summoned one of his guys, Jimmy, from the front room of the club to his office. "I'm gettin' worried that Lou didn't get the job done. Maybe she isn't as good as she thinks she is."

Jimmy answered, "Give her some time, Smokey."

Smokey lit another of his Cuban cigars and blew a smoke ring. "I want that bastard dead. After he killed my brother and then kissed him in the coffin, I want that guy deader than dead. You hear me?"

Jimmy shuffled his feet, "Maybe he's like a cat and he's got nine lives, boss. We couldn't get him, and if Lou failed, maybe nobody can whack him. I mean, his rep is that he's the best—no matter what Lou said."

Smokey blew another smoke ring. "Let me think on that. Maybe we should wait until he's back here, and then go after him. Hell, anyone I could send after him would know this town better than that dumbass island he went to. Yeah, that's what we'll do. At least for now."

Jimmy shuffled his feet again. "Sounds like a plan. But if you want me to go after him, I'd be fine takin' a trip to Hawaii."

Smokey's voice was filled with sarcasm when he responded. "I bet you would. Tell you what," Smokey continued more seriously, "you and those other buffoons I got working for me, spread the word that if anyone sees Walker back here and tells me where he is, they get fifty g's. And if they take him out, it's a quarter mil. When he steps foot in one of the boroughs, I want that to be the last step he ever takes."

"You sure?"

Smokey ground out his partially smoked cigar. "Yeah, I'm sure. Whatever it takes to get that asshole. Now get outta here, you mook. Leave me alone."

Jimmy quickly turned on his heels and left the office, while Smokey opened his humidor and lit up another Cohiba.

BACK IN MAUI

When Walker reached the row of hedges he quietly called out, "Don't shoot, it's me, Walker." When he walked behind the bushes, Sarah was sitting on the ground right where he had left her, but she had picked up the gun and was cradling it in her lap. She looked up at him with bloodshot, tear-stained, pleading eyes. "Did you see my parents? Is Mom okay?"

Walker crouched down next to Sarah, took the gun from her, and put it back in his waistband. "Listen, kid, I don't know how to sugar-coat this. Your parents didn't make it."

Sarah gasped. "What?!"

Walker went to take Sarah in his arms, but before he could, she began throwing up and between retches started screaming, "No! Oh my God! No!"

Walker began wiping the vomit off her face and mouth with his hand and then doing the best he could to clean it off by rubbing it on the grass. "I'm sorry, I don't have any tissues."

Sarah didn't hear what he said as her mind was frozen in fear and grief. She began to shake uncontrollably. Walker wrapped his arms around her, hugged her tightly to his body, and began rocking both of them. "I'm so sorry, Sarah."

She let out a piercing scream that almost deafened Walker and then fainted.

He stood up, lifted Sarah's limp body, and started carrying her down the street away from her house and toward his condo. After a few steps the cap fell off Sarah's head, so Walker awkwardly bent down, picked it up while making sure not to drop her, and put it on. Even though he knew she couldn't hear him he said, "It's yours again when you come to, kid."

Walker didn't get another block before a black sedan sped down the street and screeched to a halt alongside him. As soon as it stopped, the car doors flew open and two large, nasty-looking men who reminded

Walker of lower-NYC thugs got out and ran over to him. One positioned himself on the sidewalk to Walker's right and the other to his left. With the car blocking his access to the street there was nowhere he could go. Both men took guns out and held them next to their legs, shielding them from being seen by anyone driving past on the street.

Walker's mind raced. *These have to be the other two goons who killed Sarah's parents and the neighbors. Damn, while I'm carrying her, I have no access to my guns, or to any course of action.*

The guy to his right looked past Walker to the other man. "Is that her, the one who saw you?"

The man to Walker's left responded, "Yeah. I'm pretty sure it's her. I kind of recognize that pink top she's got on."

The first man scowled. "You gotta be sure. How sure are you?"

The second guy answered, "Not totally. I only saw someone run away. But I think it's her."

The first thug turned to Walker, "I don't know who you are, *haole*, but if you want to live to see tomorrow, you'll just hand her over to me."

"Can't do it," Walker responded. "I made a promise I'd keep her safe."

"Well," the man replied, "You're just gonna be breaking that promise, aren't you? Otherwise, you're both gonna be dead."

Walker remembered he had the Marshal identification. "Listen, pal, hold on a second. I'm a US Marshal. You don't want to be killing a Fed, do you? The ID's in my right front pocket. And we're only a block from where all the cops are at that mess you made. You shoot us here, they'll come running."

The second man reached into Walker's pocket and took out the Marshal ID and badge. "He's tellin' the truth." After he held it up for the other guy to see, he put it back in Walker's pants and then quickly patted him down and found the two guns in his waistband. "Well, looky what we got here." The man walked to the car, opened the trunk, threw the guns in, closed it again, and walked back.

The first guy scratched his head with his free hand. "I'm not sure what the hell we should do." Just then a police car turned onto their street a block away. "Shit. Let's get them both into the car and bring them to Little Mike. Let him decide how to handle this."

The second man put his gun in the small of Walker's back. "Lay her down on the back seat and you get in front. Don't try anything or I'll shoot you, cops or no cops. You got that?"

"Don't worry, bud, this isn't the day I'm choosin' to leave this planet."

The first man started moving toward the car door by the driver's seat and then got in. "Don't be so sure of that. Little Mike's gonna make that choice for you."

The second man followed behind Walker to the car's rear passenger-side door, keeping the gun barrel pressed into Walker's back. Walker clumsily opened it, fumbling with the door latch while trying not to drop Sarah. Once he got it open, he laid Sarah down across the seat. As he did, she began to wake up, and when her eyes opened a look of terror spread into them. She screamed, pointing to the guy behind Walker, "Walker, that's him! That's the man I saw."

The gun nudged into Walker as the thug said, "I thought your name's Harding. What's this Walker thing?"

Quickly thinking, Walker replied, "Walker's my nickname. I do a lot of marathons. My friends call me that."

The first man asked, "How would she know that? She a friend?"

Without missing a beat, Walker answered, "Yeah. I knew her parents pretty well."

"Then what were their names?"

Remembering what Sarah has told him earlier, Walker confidently replied, "Jean and Bob. Jean and Bob Franklin." Then he turned to Sarah. "Just sit there and try not to be scared. Everything's gonna be fine."

Sarah wanted to believe him but was trembling in fright when Walker closed the door next to her.

Walker sat down on the front passenger seat while the other man sat next to Sarah in the back. Once he closed the door he turned to Sarah. "You're not a bad looker. Maybe we can have some fun together. How old are you?"

Sarah involuntarily shrunk away from the man when he started to reach his hand out toward her. Walker pivoted to look at the back seat.

"Don't talk to him Sarah. And you, you touch her in any way, you'll be dead."

The thug pulled his arm back and gave Walker a sardonic smile. "I think you forgot who has the gun here. It ain't me that's gonna be dead when this is all over."

The driver pulled the car out from the curb and started going down the street. When he reached South Kihei Road he turned left heading south toward Wailea. After a short stretch, the road became less congested and there were fewer homes, hotels, and condo buildings lining the street.

Walker knew that if he didn't take some sort of action they'd soon be among even more members of the gang, and it would be too late to try anything. As they started to round into a curve which had a ditch on their side of the road and no oncoming cars in the opposite lane, he turned to the driver. "I got a bad itch on my leg. Got stung by a jellyfish a couple of days ago. I'm just gonna bend down a little to scratch it."

The driver kept looking straight ahead at the road. "Got stung once myself. Nasty buggers. Do what you gotta do. Just no quick moves."

Walker bent down, lifted his pant leg up a few inches, and silently took the plastic gun out of his sock. He held it in his right hand next to his leg, away from the driver's view, as he sat up. Then in one almost simultaneous series of moves he turned to face Sarah and yelled to her, "Get down on the floor. Now!" As she was dropping from the seat to the floor of the car, in one swift motion, Walker raised his right hand and shot the thug in the back seat in the middle of his forehead, and as he slumped forward against the back of the driver's seat, Walker swiveled around, grabbed onto the steering wheel with his left hand and yanked it to the right as hard as he could. The driver fought him for control, but Walker kept his hand on the wheel pulling it as far to the right as he could, and the car swerved off the road and tumbled into the ditch, turning over twice as it rolled.

Walker was prepared for what would happen, but the driver wasn't. He was thrown against the hub of the steering wheel, striking it with his breastbone, which inflated the airbag. It crushed against him and knocked out all his breath. Walker had braced his feet against the glove compartment while holding onto the strap over the door with his right hand after he discarded the plastic gun. When the car came to rest, luckily on its wheels, Walker reached over and slugged the dazed, semiconscious driver.

He turned to the back seat. "You okay?"

Sarah softly said, "I think so. My elbow hurts, but not bad."

Walker told her to stay where she was.

He got out of the car and went to the back door on the side where the man he had shot was lying. He found the thug's gun on the floor under his body, and then Walker reached over and opened the driver's door.

The driver was still unconscious when Walker put a bullet into his left temple.

Sarah shrieked when the gun went off and curled into a fetal position on the back floor. Walker hurriedly went around the car and opened the door next to her. "Get up, Sarah," he commanded in an authoritarian manner. Then he softened, "We have to get away from here before anyone sees the car."

Sarah sat upright as Walker assisted her from the vehicle. Once she was out, he put the cap back on her head, and looked at the scrape on her elbow. "That doesn't look very serious." Then took her by the arm and led her along the ditch toward Kihei, their way lit only by the light of the crescent moon. After a short walk, they came upon a path to the ocean and followed it until they reached the beach. From there they trudged on the sand toward Walker's condo without saying anything to each other until Walker broke the silence. "I'm really sorry you had to see all that, but I didn't have a choice. If I didn't kill both of them, they would have sent someone else after you. Now they won't know who you are—or me. I did what I had to do to keep the promise I made to you."

Sarah began crying again, overwhelmed by the day's events, and grabbed onto Walker's arm, squeezing it tightly. The realization of everything that had happened crept back into her thoughts. "What do I do now? What happens to me? I want my mom and dad back."

They stopped and Walker faced her. "I wish I could make that happen for you, kid, I really wish I could. But I can't. You got any relatives here? Aunts or uncles? Grandparents?"

Sarah shook her head from side to side, "No.'"

Walker was concerned by her answer. "None?"

"None," Sarah confirmed. "Mom had a brother, but he and his wife died a few years ago in a car crash. Dad had no brothers or sisters. And all my grandparents are gone. What do I do, Walker? I'm alone. I'm scared. Really scared."

She dropped down to the sand and started sobbing and shaking vigorously.

Walker sat down next to her and held her in his arms. As he did, a thought materialized. "I guess you and I might have to become each other's family now. I've got no one either, so how about I take care of you?"

"Why would you do that? We just met a few hours ago."

"I dunno. Maybe it's time for me to care about someone besides just me. What you said about me protecting you got me to thinking that I can take what I know how to do and help other people who're in danger. You know, I really believe I'd like doing that now. When I was in the Marines it was about safeguarding America. It was an honorable purpose. Since I got out, my life's been about getting rid of vermin, but mostly for other bad people. I think I'd like to go back to doing something more noble, and I'm at a point in my life where I can do whatever I want. Listen, Sarah, I've got lots of money, you can have your own room in a nice place, and in a couple of years, I'll send you to a good college. What d'ya say, kid? It beats the hell out of bein' alone. For both of us."

Sarah pulled away. "But you're a killer. How do I know you won't kill me?"

Walker reached out his hand and gently placed it on her arm. "Did you read about the Knights of the Round Table in school?"

Sarah nodded, "Yes."

Walker continued, "Then think of me as your Lancelot. He went out and killed people to protect Guinevere. I would never harm you, kid."

Sarah hugged Walker and cried profusely on his shoulder.

Once she calmed down, she said, "Walker, I don't know what else

I'd do or where I'd go except for you. But can I see my mom and dad? I want to say goodbye to them."

"I don't know if that can happen, Sarah. Once the police know where you are, they'll probably try to put you in a foster home. If that's what you want, I'll go along with it. But if you'd rather stay with me, then Sarah Franklin has to disappear. We'll get your hair cut and maybe turn you into a blond like most of the girls I've seen around here, buy you a bunch of new clothes, get you a different name, move somewhere else on the islands, and I'll enroll you in a new school there. As far as the police'll know, you're gone or maybe the gang got you and you're dead somewhere. After a while they'll stop looking for you. I know how cops work. Believe me."

"I want to stay with you, Walker, not be with some people I don't know."

"That's what I was hoping you'd say, so starting right now, how about you're Sarah Harding? You can call me Walker, but since I've got no other friends here, to everyone else I'm Fred or Harding. That work for you?"

Sarah nodded in agreement.

"Good," Walker acknowledged, "Now, let's get to my condo and get you settled in. I guess it was serendipity that it's got two bedrooms."

Sarah smiled for the first time since Walker had met her. "Serendipity? Big word, but a good one. Nice."

Sarah and Walker trekked down the beach with her holding tightly onto his arm as she once again cried tears of sorrow for her parents and the life she would never be going back to, while at the same time not feeling the chest-gripping weight of being an orphan with no one to take care of her.

And Walker was surprised at how much he was looking forward to having someone he could care for and nurture in his life.

Before Walker could ruminate too long on those thoughts his cell rang. "Walker, it's Junior."

"I didn't expect to hear from you again tonight. What're you doin' up this late?"

"I just got a call from Marky Weiss. You remember him?"

"Sure do. He helped out your dad with that bookie. Good guy."

"Marky called me from an all-nighter poker game he was at over in Hell's Kitchen. He told me that a guy walked in and announced that Smokey Challow—you know, the guy who owns the Bizzazz Club—put a bounty on you. Fifty big ones if anyone spots you and two hundred and fifty if they take you out. I knew you'd want to know."

Walker stopped walking and looked at Sarah. He decided to be careful what he said to Junior. "Thanks for the info. I think I understand what's going on now. Challow's the guy I was supposed to take care of, so he's gotta be the one who set me up. I gotta give him credit for thinkin' up somethin' like that, but at least I know what I've gotta do now. I don't wanna keep lookin' over my shoulder when I know how to take care of the problem. Keep me posted if you hear anything else, Junior. I'll probably take a trip back there sometime soon. Just not right now."

When the call ended, Sarah looked at Walker questioningly. "Why would you have to look over your shoulder, Walker?" Then she added with a quiver of concern in her voice, "You're not leaving me, are you? You said you'd be taking a trip soon."

Walker folded his arms across his chest. "Now listen to me, young lady. You have nothing to worry about. I will have to go back East sometime, but only for a day or two, and it won't be for a while. When I go, I'll make sure you're not left alone. I'll have one of my friends come stay with you—probably Junior. You'll like him, his father was my mentor. And as for looking over my shoulder, I told you I used to go after bad guys. Well, one of them tried to hurt me, just like those thugs tried to hurt you, but he couldn't and I'm gonna make sure he never does. You okay with that?"

Sarah nodded, "I guess so." She grabbed onto Walker's arm, and they started walking to the condo.

As they trudged along on the sand, Walker asked her, "You want to stay around here or go to one of the other islands? The choice is yours."

That took Sarah by surprise. "Really? The choice is mine?"

Walker answered, "Yep. Wherever you want to live is where we'll live."

Sarah thought for a moment before replying. "Can I have a couple of days to think about it?"

"Absolutely. Just make sure you pick a place with a good school, 'cause you're gonna have to get into a classroom soon and start preparin' for college. No kid of mine's gonna be uneducated."

Sarah squeezed Walker's arm, and when she did, he turned to her, "Hey' I've got an idea. You know what I said about Lancelot—"

She looked up at him. "Yes. I won't forget that."

He continued. "—and how I can use what I do to help other people."

"That too," Sarah confirmed.

"Well," Walker continued, "I've got a great idea how to combine the two. I'm gonna call myself the White Knight. I'll be a knight in shining armor for people in trouble and being threatened."

A big grin spread across Sarah's face. "You're already *my* knight in shining armor. That's perfect. I love it, Walker."

"Me too," he agreed. "I like it a lot."

Before either of them could say anything else, they looked up, saw that they had reached the Oceanview Resort, and went inside.

JEFFERY DEAVER

THE LADY IN MY LIFE

Upper New York Bay—a.k.a. New York Harbor—is considered by many to be the best natural Harbor in the world.

It can also be among the most beautiful, as was the case today. The water was gunmetal, and the breeze was teasing up whitecaps. A container ship, massive, like a thirty-story building in recline, eased gracefully west, aiming toward the New Jersey docks, where the many-colored trailers would be lifted off and sent to depots around the country, and new ones seated on the vessel for a journey to who-knew-where.

Taking it all in was Miguel Torres, sitting on a bench in North Shore Waterfront Esplanade Park, the northern tip of Staten Island. He was eating his lunch, which he had made himself. It was a tuna-salad sandwich, dressed with cheese and pickles. The bread was homemade white.

Baking was a hobby of his (he could not make a casserole or cook a roast, but flour and yeast were ever at his command). He was drinking hot chocolate from a cup that he had unscrewed from a lengthy green thermos.

He was a compact man with thick, trimmed black hair and a matching mustache. His face was handsome enough to be that of a model. He was five feet eight inches tall. And muscular, thanks not to a gym (he had not been to one in five years) but to his profession of landscaper.

Presently, as often, he was mesmerized as he gazed over the water at the distant, ever-impressive fortress of buildings in lower Manhattan, at Governor's and Liberty Islands, at the no-nonsense docks and warehouses of Brooklyn and, to his left, the bristling cranes of New Jersey's industrial backbone: the cranes that lifted, loaded, and offloaded the containers he'd been thinking of moments ago.

He stretched. Felt a bone pop.

Tired . . .

The alarm had cried out at 4:30 a.m. and, after rolling groggily from bed, he'd had a breakfast of cold tamales and coffee and then driven to Mr. Whittaker's house, a nice brick two-story in Tudor style. Miguel had been hired to "make it nice for spring." Mr. Whittaker was a recent widower and Miguel had learned that his wife had been the gardener in the family. The retired businessman himself didn't have the heart to putter in the yard, given his loss.

Miguel was attending to the man's flower beds, in sore need of hand-weeding (the only way to do it) and nutrients. He still had eight, nine hours of work to make the yard beautiful once more, beautiful in the way that only living plants could accomplish.

A thought landed like a determined bee on a flower—how different was his life here, compared with that back home. The desert had its beauty but could not compare with the endlessly pulsating plane of water that stretched out before him.

This place was very special. Miguel often dreamed—waking and otherwise—about owning a house with a water view like this. There were a number of such residences available, of course, overlooking the Harbor in all of the boroughs, except Queens and the Bronx. But affording one was another matter. And Miguel Torres had another requirement that limited his ability to find his perfect residence: he would never live in an apartment or condo, water vista or not. He thrived on soil and grass and plants. Which meant that prices for even the most modest of places that would meet his standards started over a million. His age was thirty-two. Over a beer at night, or coffee after work, or hot chocolate at lunch he calculated that by the time he saved enough to buy, he would be seventy-four, depending of course on the undependable real estate market of New York City.

Of course, miracles could happen. But for the time being, he was content to stroll along the Esplanade anytime he wished. And for free.

The park was crowded with people who'd flocked here to enjoy the beautiful early-April day, one of the most temperate of the year so far. Curious by nature, Miguel gazed about. To his right, on the other side of a thick stand of boxwood, was a cluster of three or four people engaged in an animated conversation. He couldn't help but play the eavesdropping game.

In front of him on the concrete walkway, joggers trotted past. Most were frowning. In pain? He laughed. He could tell them about muscle pain—after eight-hour days spent doing what he did.

To Miguel's left, on an adjoining bench, a businessman had doffed his jacket and rolled up his shirt sleeves. He sloughed back and gazed upward, as if praying for a tan.

Miguel took in the Mixmaster blend of all of the sounds cascading, swirling, descending upon him—and the laughter, the caw of gulls, the slap of water, the voices . . .

He remained motionless, a man lost in thought, for ten minutes, then rose and tossed his trash into a nearby bin, much to the disappointment—and ire—of a large gull.

Returning to the sidewalk, he paused momentarily and glanced into the Harbor, then walked steadily from the park.

Miguel Torres had work to do.

———

The next morning, he was on Paxton Street, which was tucked between the Brighton Heights and Stapleton Heights neighborhoods of Staten Island.

He wore what he usually did on the job: jeans and a flannel shirt—today gray and blue—over a black T-shirt. Today was summer scented and even warmer than yesterday and he'd left his jacket in the truck.

Much of the huge island, one of the five boroughs, or counties, of New York City, had been gentrified. These particular blocks had not been—but they hadn't needed much spiffing. The houses were old but masterfully and solidly built. They were kept up well, and little trim was in need of painting. Most had decent-sized yards, both front and back. Miguel was presently hard at work, engaged in his most effective sales effort: walking from house to house and offering the occupants one of his cards or leaving one on the doorstep if no one was home. If he did have the chance to meet the homeowner and they were willing to listen, he'd offer a brief description of what he might do to make their property more beautiful.

And safer.

As was the case now.

He was standing in front of a single-family home in what was called gingerbread style, the gray siding like fish scales, the roof shingled with dark red asphalt. The windows were of beveled glass, the doorknob and hinges polished brass. He guessed the structure was one hundred years old.

The small front yard consisted of carelessly mowed and under-fertilized grass. Some dirt beds were home to a few shrubs and flowing plants, looking none too healthy.

What took his attention, though, was the dominant element of the property: a towering oak, sixty feet high. He knew the rate at which hardwood trees grew and he supposed that it had been planted as a sapling when the construction of the house was completed.

Miguel walked to the front door, rang the bell.

He heard footsteps and a moment later a woman opened the door. She was about his age, maybe a bit older, and had a narrow, striking face and abundant blond hair tied up in a ponytail.

"Yes?" she asked. If she was cautious about a stranger at the door, she gave no evidence of it.

"Hi. Good morning." He had studied English from his grammar school days, and he had only a faint accent.

He offered his card.

> *A-One Landscaping*
> *Miguel Torres*
> *Trees, plantings, irrigation, stump removal, carting*
> *Licensed and Bonded.*

She glanced at it, then behind him, at his truck, a twenty-two foot Chevy 6500, which he kept in immaculate shape (the cleanliness was part of his sales pitch—to demonstrate his responsibility and the care he took in his work). The woman was in jeans and a close-fitting light-blue blouse. Her necklace was a cross. So, most likely a Catholic, like him.

"Oh, I'm renting. I can give you the number of the owner. He'd be the one to talk to about any work."

She wasn't from Staten Island. There's a unique way native islanders talk. Her sentences would have diminished in volume at the end and trailed off to silence. And "owner" would likely have been "owniz" and "number" "numbaz." Locals often added an "s" sound to singular words.

She also had a faint accent that was definitely not from the Island: He believed it was southern.

Miguel said, "Sure. I can call him. But I wanted to point out something. There's a problem." He turned to the oak. "That branch is about to come down."

The twenty-foot limb drooped over her SUV, a black Honda, which was showing a dusting of pollen from the very oak tree that was threatening to cave in its roof.

"I never noticed it." She stepped out onto the front porch and studied the branch, which was about a foot in diameter where it had begun splitting off from the trunk.

"What happened?"

"Could've been anything. Wind or that ice storm last winter. Maybe age. The tree's healthy otherwise."

She turned to him. They were about eye to eye, his deep brown, hers a glowing blue.

"I'm Katherine. With a K." She noted his card. "And it's your company. You're Miguel?"

"With an M."

A beat of a moment and she laughed.

They shook hands. He was always careful about this. His palms were calloused and very strong. But she didn't shy, and her grip was firm too. When their hands retreated, she didn't look away but scanned his face for a moment.

He too held her eyes, with a cocked head, then turned to the front of the property. "I'm thinking this could be a nice yard."

"The owner doesn't do very much. Obviously."

"I wouldn't mind getting a contract." His eyes returned to hers. "Let me propose something. I'll take care of the branch for nothing. If you could tell the owner about it and give him my number . . . What do you think?"

She debated for a moment. Then: "Well, you can't beat the price. A deal. I'll move the Honda."

Katherine turned and with her left hand reached up and pulled some keys off a hook just inside the door. She was not wearing a wedding or engagement ring.

She backed into the street, then parked in front of his truck.

Miguel got his climbing gear from the back bed and one of the smaller chainsaws.

"You mind if I watch?"

He laughed. "Won't be as dramatic as a hundred-foot redwood coming down. But be my guest."

After mounting the climbing spikes on his boots, he slung the canvas strap around the tree and clipped it to the rings on his utility belt. The chainsaw went over his shoulder. He flipped the strap upward so that it encircled the trunk about three feet above his head. He pulled it taut and, flexing his arms and climbing with the spiked boots, moved upward. He kept repeating the process until he was at the branch.

He glanced back and saw her sitting on the porch studying him. She called, "Like Spiderman."

He chuckled and pulled on goggles and yellow ear protectors then fired up the chainsaw. It took only four strategic cuts for gravity to take over and the limb fell to the ground as undramatically as Miguel had promised.

He now descended and removed the climbing gear. He untucked and removed his flannel shirt, folded and set it on a boxwood nearby. The T-shirt revealed his muscular frame and from the corner of his eye he saw Katherine swiftly study his torso and then look back to the branch.

He tugged the saw to life once more and within a few minutes the limb had become six separate logs.

Removing the goggles and earmuffs, he asked, "You want it stacked for firewood? It'll have to dry for a few months."

"I won't be here much longer than that myself. I don't think the fireplace works anyway."

"I'll get rid of it."

In Staten Island homeowners can leave their own yard waste at curb-side for pickup, but what professional landscapers generate has to be hauled away by them. One by one, Miguel squatted, lifted the wood, and threw it in the bed of his truck. Each weighed about fifty pounds, he guessed, but they were nothing for him.

"Where will you take it?" Katherine asked.

"We have approved dump sites. Not too far."

He wiped his forehead with his shirt, then replaced it on the shrub.

"Would you like some water?"

"Sure. Thanks."

Inside, the house was quite nice. *Majestuosa*—stately—was the word that came to mind.

It featured wood-paneled walls, leaded-glass panels in the doors, red-and-black oriental carpets, and more brass fixtures.

"You mind if I wash my hands?"

She pointed to a bathroom and Miguel stepped inside. Like in many old houses there were separate hot and cold faucets, with the hot too searing to use alone. He filled the basin, washed with a lavender foam soap, and then rinsed off in cold water.

He joined Katherine in the spacious kitchen, where she moved a stack of papers off the high-top island. This room seemed to serve as an office.

"Take a seat," she said, indicating the stools.

He hesitated briefly and then sat. While customers sometimes offered him water, none had ever asked him to sit down; they usually seemed eager that he finish his drink and leave.

"Or coffee?"

This had never been offered either.

"No, just water's fine."

She got a glass from a cabinet, added ice, and filled it from the faucet. He wondered if she'd sit too, but no. She remained standing and sipped from a coffee mug.

After a moment of silence, he asked, "You're only here for a while?"

Katherine replied, "I work in IT—you know, internet. A four-month assignment. It's usually cheaper to rent a house than pay for an extended-stay hotel." She looked him up and down again. "You done landscaping all your life?"

"No, no. Started five years ago, when I came here from Mexico."

"I only ask because . . ." Her voice trailed off, and not because of a Staten Island dialect. She seemed to regret where her comment had been going. About his excellent English and grammar, he guessed.

"Down there I wore a suit and tie." His shoulders rose and fell. "But my degree didn't mean much here, so I started my own company."

"That's not fair." She was frowning.

"I thought so at first, but I like this better. Much better. I'm my own boss. Outside, working with my hands."

"Why'd you leave?"

His face darkened "Too dangerous. The cartels. A new president comes in. 'Oh, I'll clean it up. I'll make the country safe . . .' A joke. They never do. I brought my parents and sister too. They're in California."

"But you didn't go there?"

"No. I like New York. It's special."

"It is. Very special. I'll be sad to leave when the job's over."

She refilled the coffee mug, which did not seem to need refilling. "You mentioned your family . . . Anybody else come with you?"

"No. Just us." A pause. "There *was* a woman I was seeing." He shrugged. "She could have come. But she wanted to stay. I can't blame her. It's the hardest thing in the world, leaving your family. She couldn't do it."

He thought about Consuela a lot. He tried not to but that usually proved to be impossible.

"You'll meet somebody here."

"I'm in no hurry. My mother always says, 'Just wait and see what fate has in store for you.'"

"That sounds a little . . . can I say? Ominous."

"I always thought that too."

They shared a laugh and their eyes met once more. Was she offering a flirt, perhaps an invitation of some sort?

He wasn't sure.

But what he did know for certain was that *he* was.

The spell broke. He finished the water and rose. "I should go."

Together, they walked to the front door and onto the porch. She glanced out into the yard. "That other work you wanted to do here. Why don't you just come back and do it? If the landlord won't pay I'll get my company to."

"Well . . ."

"No. Really. It's too nice a yard to look like it does now. Gets prettified, it'll be nice to sit on the steps and have a glass of wine."

"'Prettified.' That's a new one to me."

Katherine's eyes were very much the color of Upper New York Bay on a sunny summer afternoon.

Another silence. Neither moved.

He came a second away from easing forward to see how receptive she'd be to a kiss. He sensed: a lot.

But then he told himself firmly: Careful there.

Which he modified to: Take. Your. Time.

"I can start tomorrow?" asked Miguel.

"Tomorrow would be perfect."

———

Overnight the temperature had dropped, and it was now ten degrees cooler than yesterday. Overcast and windier too.

The oak, one limb less, swayed, and the budding leaves rustled.

Miguel hit the doorbell button and just a moment later he was aware of footsteps approaching.

Katherine opened the door. She was smiling. He reciprocated. And, though it seemed like an odd gesture, he stuck his hand out. She gripped it firmly and the contact lingered.

He couldn't stop his eyes from sweeping down and then back up. Her outfit was of gray, shimmery cloth, silky. Almost like pajamas.

No, *exactly* like pajamas.

"Morning," he said.

"*Buenos dias.*"

He laughed. Her pronunciation was terrible. "So. With the wind, I checked the tree again. All good. You're safe from falling branches." He noted she'd kept it parked on the street overnight.

"My hero."

"I've got lime and fertilizer and some acid for the hydrangeas. Rose food too. Where would you like me to start?"

A frown, a tilt of her head. "Here." She took his right hand and put it on her breast.

Miguel was motionless for a moment. One had to be careful nowadays of course, but if this didn't qualify as "consent" he didn't know what might. So he slid his other hand around her waist to the small of her back and pulled her to him, kissing her hard.

She gripped his lips with her teeth. Then opened her mouth and kissed him back just as passionately.

Katherine turned and led him into the hallway, closing the door behind them. Then, still gripping his hand firmly led him into the bedroom. The lace curtains were partially open, and you could see a portion of the gardens surrounding the backyard. They were in even worse shape than those in the front.

Miguel Torres didn't care.

———

He opened his eyes to find her dressing.

It was noon. Two hours had passed since he'd arrived, and only the past fifteen or twenty minutes had been devoted to sleep.

She noticed he was awake and smiled.

He did too.

And told himself not to think of Consuela. Though he did, concluding that, as good as such times had been with her, none had risen to this level.

He sat up, swung his feet to the floor. Sipped from the bottle of water on the bedside table. She'd set it there while he dozed.

Katherine walked close and kissed him. She whispered, "Sleepyhead."

"I'm awake now."

She glanced down. "You certainly are."

He lifted an eyebrow. It was an invitation. To accept or reject as she wished.

She clicked her tongue and her face registered disappointment. "I've got an associate who'll be here in ten minutes."

"Well," Miguel offered, "maybe tomorrow."

She frowned.

He shook his head.

She said, "What's wrong with tonight?"

His answer was a firm kiss.

Miguel rose to wash up and dress while she made the bed.

Together they walked into the kitchen.

"Coffee now?"

He'd been just a water-drinking handyman yesterday. His status had changed.

"Black."

As she poured two cups the doorbell sounded.

"That'd be Tim," she said, handing him the brew. He took it and sipped. Strong. He liked it.

She walked to the front door and opened it, letting inside a stocky man in his thirties, dressed in jeans, a white dress shirt, and a navy blazer. He was blond, his hair longish. He carried a backpack on one shoulder, a computer bag over the other. It dangled at his side like a large purse.

He said to Katherine, "Morning," though his eyes were on Miguel.

She introduced him and added, "He's a friend."

Miguel had wondered if she'd say, "My gardener."

"Nice to meet you."

Miguel's impression, however, was that he didn't feel it was so very nice. A smile was on his face, but it was one of *those* smiles—of questionable DNA.

The men gripped hands. Tim's fingers were long but were the digits of a computer person, not an outdoor worker.

Miguel was careful not to exert too much pressure.

She poured Tim some coffee, as well, and added cream and sugar.

He took several sips and then set the cup down on the island and opened the computer bag. He extracted his laptop, a big one, the seventeen-inch model. He set this on the kitchen table, tugged open the lid, and booted the Dell up. After loading some documents or diagrams—Miguel couldn't see clearly—he scanned the screen and pointed to some portion of it. Katherine bent down and read.

She said, "Good. They delivered on time. We're right on schedule."

Tim nodded but his face didn't register the same satisfaction hers did. Which had nothing to do with their project. Tim was jealous.

As Tim looked over Katherine, Miguel studied him. He was not an attractive man, but round and fidgety, unathletic—a high school student who'd kept waiting to flower, to slip from nerd to cool, but had never been able to get beyond the video-gaming, candy-sneaking, girl-ogling years.

His crush on Katherine would run deep and he knew she would always be interested in the Miguels of the world. He would have talents, important ones—like making sure things ran "right on schedule"—but that was different.

Tim, of course, couldn't resent her, not openly, given the infatuation and the obvious fact that she was his superior.

So he'd suck it up when on the subject of Miguel Torres and offer the smile that perhaps he honestly believed would really be taken for one.

He was just wondering whether he should tell her he was going to get to work on the yard when her phone rang, and she took a call. As she listened a frown blossomed on her face.

"Well, that's not going to work. How would that work?" Her voice had an edge he hadn't heard before. She held her hand over the phone and said to Tim, "The trucking company. An accident. They can't do it."

Tim was frowning. He stammered, "They . . . they have to."

She said, "It's not happening. Their other trucks're on the road." She returned to the call. "You'll just have to find another way. We've paid you twenty percent . . . I don't want the money back. I want the shipment delivered like you're contracted to do . . . No, I don't want you jobbing it out. We vetted *you*. We don't have time to screen anybody else. Oh, never mind." She hit disconnect and it seemed she regretted not being able to slam a landline receiver down into a cradle.

She stared at the floor for a moment, her beautiful face registering dismay. She looked to Tim. "So. What do we do? They have to go on board this afternoon. There're no options."

He muttered, "We have to call corporate."

"Oh, great. I can't *wait* to have that conversation."

Miguel asked, "What do you have to be delivered?"

"Computer racks for crude oil tankers' navigation systems."

Tim added, "They're algorithms that measure wind, current, depth of water, draft, dimensions of ships, a hundred other things. They find the most fuel-efficient routes whatever the seas are like."

Katherine was staring at the computer screen. "The contract . . . They *have* to be dropped at the boat we've chartered. Today. In the next few hours."

She looked to Tim, who grimaced.

Miguel asked, "Where are they? And where do they have to go?"

She waved to the computer. "They were just dropped off at a warehouse in Brooklyn. Red hook. We have a boat at Emerson Dock on Staten Island. That's where they're going."

"I know it," Miguel said. "How big are these things?"

The two regarded each other. Tim said, "Probably fifty pounds."

"How many?"

"Twelve. What are you . . . ?"

"I can do it," Miguel offered.

Tim said, "What, in a landscaping truck?"

Miguel looked him over closely. "The suspension's just like any other thirty-footer."

"But—"

"No," Katherine said, smiling. "I like it."

"Well," Tim said slowly, "How much'd you charge?"

His face suggested he did not want another man to save the day and impress fair Katherine.

Miguel thought for a moment, calculating in his head. Staten Island to Brooklyn and back again. "Make it two fifty."

Katherine laughed. Tim stared at him. She was the one who said, "The job we contracted for is two thousand. That's what we'd pay you."

Miguel lifted an eyebrow. "I think I'm in the wrong line of work."

Tim said to her, "You sure? I mean . . . Security?"

"You have any other options? Those ships sail without the modules, they cancel our contract and buy from Allied Atlantic or Bermuda Systems."

The man nodded.

He gave Miguel the address of the warehouse where he was to pick up the modules and the specific pier at Emerson Dock where the boat to deliver the products to the ships was located. The captain and crew were on their way. If they weren't there by the time he arrived he should stow them on board, in the hold.

"Don't just leave them on the pier. We couldn't afford to have them stolen."

Miguel gave a laugh and said with some pride, "Staten Island's not like *some* places around here. But we're still New York City." He said he'd be sure to leave them out of sight.

"You're a lifesaver," she said warmly and with obvious gratitude.

There was a beat of a moment as he wondered how she would say goodbye to him.

But there was no hesitation on her part. She walked straight up and kissed him on the mouth.

This was right in front of Tim, who tried unsuccessfully to mask the irritation, if not anger, at his rival.

Miguel said, "I have one condition."

"Name it." She offered a seductive smile.

"I get that rose food on the bushes as soon as I'm back. Can't wait another day."

———

An easy job.

The drive to the Red Hook warehouse took thirty minutes. Once there, he displayed to a bored manager the bill of lading that Katherine had printed out. The man's spirits improved considerably, and he grew more than happy to help load the *cartos* when Miguel held up two twenties and a ten.

Fifty or so minutes later he arrived at the dock. It took no time at all to find the ship, or boat, or whatever you call a craft that was about thirty feet long. It seemed old but the construction was solid, the wood varnished and clean. Like Katherine's rental, the fixtures were polished brass. The captain and crew weren't present. He borrowed a hand truck from a sailor on another craft and three at a time wheeled the cartons to the side of the vessel. He lifted them to the deck, which was a few feet above the pier and then, jumping on board, carried them down into the hold.

He had a thought and laughed. Of *course* that's what the large diesel-smelling space was called—because that was where the cargo was "held."

After returning the hand cart he walked back to his Chevy and looked out over the Harbor, gray and dotted with more whitecaps than the other day, but magnificent still.

He started the truck and drove back toward Paxton Street.

Thinking once again:

I'm in the wrong line of work . . .

———

Katherine and Tim had been joined by three other men.

They were pale of complexion and in good shape. There was a military air about them, an impression aided by the fact that they wore similar outfits—tan tops and slacks. They almost appeared to be uniforms. Their hairstyle was similar too: cropped short. He wondered if they had been soldiers.

"It went well?" Tim asked.

"Fine. They're loaded. Inside. When I left, the crew still hadn't gotten there."

"Not a problem," said Tim. He nodded at one of the three men, who pulled out his phone and quickly made a call. Something was different about Tim. He was more confident than earlier. Much less of a nerd. Katherine might be in charge, but Tim was a strong second in command. The three newcomers were respectful of him. Maybe even intimidated.

Miguel spotted another difference too. Looking past the hallway, Miguel noted that the bed was no longer made. The blazer that Tim had worn lay on the chair beside it.

And Katherine had changed clothes yet again, now wearing a skirt and a blue cotton blouse.

She took in his face, aware that he understood what had happened. She handed off a look that was very different from the others she'd offered over the past two days. It was the glance you would give to a busboy passing you in a restaurant.

Then Tim said to the trio of men, "All right."

They turned and, before Miguel could even swivel and start for the door, they were on him.

"Wait . . . what . . . ?"

This had all been planned—like choreography.

One pulled a pistol from his back pocket and pointed it at Miguel, who blinked. His eyes turned to Katherine. She gave him another restaurant-help glance and then took a packet of alcohol wipes and began scouring the laptop—the keys, the top, the sides, the battery charger. She nodded.

With the gun still on him, the other two dragged him to the laptop and forced his hands open. They pressed his fingertips onto the keys and parts of the computer she'd scrubbed.

Resisting was impossible, even if he hadn't been at gunpoint; the two planting his fingerprints were strong as bodybuilders.

"What is this? I don't understand!"

Tim pulled on latex gloves and sat at the computer. He began typing.

Miguel turned to Katherine, his eyes imploring her to explain.

"We're patriots." She shrugged. "Government's a perversion. It's grown into a cancerous behemoth that's destroying true values of what America should be. It's driving us toward the poison of globalism. We're not going to put up with that. We won't tolerate foreigners or their influence, and we won't tolerate a *government* that supports them."

"Spare me bullshit speeches. What did you get me into?"

Tim said absently, "Those cartons?"

Miguel whispered, "Not computer racks. They're bombs or chemical weapons, aren't they?"

"Twelve hundred pounds of C-4," Katherine said as she watched Tim—her boyfriend, her lover—type away at the keyboard.

"There never was a delivery problem. You saw 'carting' on my business card, you saw my truck, and planned to set me up." Then he frowned. "A suicide mission . . . Ah, no, the boat. It's remote controlled."

Tim didn't bother to confirm. "Launching it now." He hit return.

Glancing at the screen, Miguel could see a window of a bobbing image, a live feed. It would be from a camera mounted to the front of the boat. Slowly at first it cruised forward, aiming away from shore into the Harbor.

He closed his eyes briefly. He opened them and raged to Katherine, "You set me up! I'm the one on video picking up the packages and loading them on the boat." He gave a sour laugh. "And my fingerprints." A nod at the computer. "It'll look like I was steering the boat!"

Nobody had anything to say.

Miguel Torres had merely stated the obvious.

"And that?"

Katherine looked his way to see what he meant.

He was staring into the bedroom.

She shrugged.

Which meant that, obviously, she needed to seal the deal. And, with a man, what better way to cloud his judgment and make sure he didn't speculate too much about the curious job—picking up cartons for a big computer operation and loading them onto a small boat all by himself.

Miguel looked them over. "What exactly is your point? I mean, *I* wasn't born here. I immigrated legally and I've worked every day of my life in this country. I love America. I'm a citizen."

"Not a real one," muttered one of the tan uniformed thugs.

The word that came to Miguel's mind was: Nazi.

He asked, "And what's going to happen to me? I'll kill myself?"

Why even bother? Of course that was the plan.

"What's your target? A container ship from Brazil or China or Europe?"

"Something much better than that," Katherine said.

"Are you going to tell me?"

Tim said, "We'll let you watch."

Miguel said, "Planes and drones'd be monitored. A small boat in the Harbor. Nobody would pay it any attention."

He glanced at the three clones, then asked Tim and Katherine, "Where are you all from?"

Tim said, "Outside of Birmingham." He glanced to Miguel. "And, okay, just to let you know: we think some of you are okay."

"What?" Miguel whispered.

"Somebody's got to cut the grass and iron the sheets and fix the roofs. Stay in your place and it's all good."

Miguel stared back, his face expressionless. Was the man taunting him? Or serious?

Katherine said to the Hitler Youth, "Let's get on with it. I want to be on the road in a half hour."

While the gunman kept his pistol thrust forward, the other two walked to the stairway, where a length of clothesline lay on the landing. One end was a loop, like an impromptu noose. The other end one of them tied to the banister, so that the loop ended about seven feet off the floor.

"I'm going to hang myself," he whispered.

Both Katherine and Tim were staring at the screen as his long, weak fingers typed commends which ended up as directives to the ship's rudder.

The two placed a chair under the noose and walked Miguel toward it. He looked back at her. "Ah, Katherine . . . Katherine . . ."

There was something about his tone that caught her attention.

Her ocean-blue eyes stared into his brown, as he shook his head slowly. His face would have to be revealing a hint of sadness—though for her, not himself.

"Oh, no," she whispered.

He nodded.

It was then that the FBI tactical team smashed open the door with a battering ram and a dozen agents with machine guns and pistols at the ready charged into the house, screaming—literally—for everyone to drop to the floor and keep their hands in sight.

The alternative, the agents made clear, was that they'd be shot where they stood.

The quintet quickly complied.

———

The terrorists had been carted away to federal detention in lower Manhattan, and a crime scene team was scouring the house.

Miguel Torres stood outside with the lead special agent on the case, a tall, dark-skinned man of around fifty. His short, white hair was distinguished. Despite the tough job Special Agent William Nichols would have, his eyes sparkled constantly. He asked, "The calvary cut it too close?"

Miguel replied, "I had every faith in you. If for no other reason than you'd have a lot of explaining to do to your attorney general if your confidential informant got himself hanged."

He hadn't in fact been too worried. Nichols had assured him that there would be two dozen agents surrounding the house and listening to every word uttered inside, through the microphone sewed into Miguel's pockets.

They would want to get as much incriminating information on the cell as they could, but of course, since the plan was to kill Miguel, at the least overt action or command to do so, the tactical team would rescue him.

Already the press was gathering, but other agents and NYPD officers were keeping them back. Miguel knew there would be a press conference at some point. Hero though he was, he would not participate. For one thing, he was a reclusive man by nature. For another, it was obviously not a wise idea to be identified as the man who stopped a terrorist attack by the infamous Patriot Enforcers Militia. Five had been arrested, but Nichols told him that the outfit had a half dozen branches and numbed close to fifty members. Once the full extent of the plot was known that number would shrink considerably. But even then, anonymity was the better course.

"I think this is the fastest operation we've ever put together," Nichols said and he stepped away to take a phone call.

Fast indeed. It was only two days ago—at his lunch on the Esplanade—that he had overheard the conversation among Katherine, Tim, and several others, probably the three Nazis, who were unaware of Miguel's presence and assumed no one was within earshot. It was this crowd on which he was eavesdropping.

They were on the waterfront to plot out the route their explosive boat would take to its target.

They were not the most brilliant of perpetrators; they should have come up with code words for what they actually said, like "transporting the C-4," "explosion," "body count," and "the day after tomorrow."

He had also heard Katherine—tell the others to meet that night at her house, which was apparently the base of the operation.

After disposing of his lunch trash, Miguel had followed her home to the house on Paxton Street. It was not far from the water, and he could trail on foot.

He had then gone straight to FBI headquarters in Manhattan with the story and was ushered immediately into Nichols's office. He was the head of a joint FBI/NYPD antiterror task force. He convened a number of officers and together, in the space of only a few hours, they had concocted a take-down plan, Miguel himself suggesting that he work his way into the cell to learn exactly what they were up to.

He had an idea of how he would do so: When he'd followed Katherine back to her house, he'd noted a large oak in the front yard. That night, he'd snuck onto the property with a hand saw, climbed the tree, and cut through much of the branch that overhung the driveway.

The next day he'd gone to the house and offered to take down the dangerously dangling limb for free.

But meeting her was only part of the plan. There was an important refinement. At the meeting on the Esplanade he'd heard them talk about transporting the explosives from a warehouse to a dock but were worried about exposing themselves to CCTV cameras. So when he made his offer to cut the branch, he'd proffered his card, which stated that among other services he provided carting.

This got him inside the cell.

He didn't share with Special Agent Nichols that a bit more had unfolded between him and Katherine. Miguel understood that she was using the time in bed to snare him. What she didn't know was that he was using her too; it had been a long time since he'd been with Consuela.

This morning he had picked up the explosives at the warehouse in Brooklyn but instead of delivering them to the dock right away he'd made a fast stop—a garage where NYPD and BATF bomb squad teams rendered the devices safe. He'd then continued on and loaded them onto the boat per the terrorists' instructions.

Nichols finished his phone call and disconnected. "The mayor wants to meet you. The governor too. I told them you're in deep cover. They're going to send you a letter or something." Eyes dancing, he added, "Maybe an Amazon gift certificate. That's a joke."

"How long will they go away for?"

"Attempted murder, attempted destruction of federal property, conspiracy, maybe sedition . . . I guess fifty years."

Miguel nodded with satisfaction.

Nichols gave a laugh. "Figured you'd left your prior life behind, did you?"

One of the reasons the agent and his team had so readily agreed to Miguel's suggestion that he go undercover was his old job in Mexico: He was a senior detective investigating the Chihuahua and Sinaloa drug cartels and a political liaison officer.

After the assassination attempt number three down there, Miguel had said enough was enough—they'd get him sooner or later. With the help of the US authorities he'd worked with in Texas, he'd immigrated, along with his parents, his sister, and her husband.

The issue of Consuela Ramirez's joining him had never arisen; it was she who'd set him up for the third hit.

And so America became his new home.

Miguel noted that the reporters were antsy, like racehorses just before the gates open. They wanted their facts. Or if not facts then something that approximated them.

"Have a thought, Agent Nichols."

The man lifted an eyebrow.

Miguel continued, "You'll need my statement, but I'll come into your office tonight."

"Fine. But why?"

A nod toward the press. "They'll be wondering what I'm doing here, how I'm connected. You act like there's nothing I can tell you and walk away. I'll get back to work—I'm just the gardener who happened to be here, taking care of the grounds."

"Smart. Good plan." The agent did as he suggested.

Miguel walked to his truck, collected what he needed. A few reporters asked a question or two but he simply frowned and said with a thick accent, "Nobody tell me nothing."

He returned to the yard.

Yes, it was true that this was a good cover to keep him out of the story.

But just as important, vines threatened to strangle the camelias, and the beds of gypsophila, delphiniums, and buddleia had clearly not been treated with lime in forever.

Those were both sins, and Miguel Torres would make certain they were remedied as soon as possible.

———

The next day, having tidied up the grounds on Paxton Street and finished "prettifying" the beds at Mr. Whittaker's, Miguel was once again eating lunch on the Esplanade—this time a meat loaf sandwich on rye, one of his signature loaves.

His name had successfully been kept out of the press, though of course he had shared with his parents and sister the entire story.

"*Mio dios*," his mother had gasped. "What a risk you took!"

He assured her that he'd been under the careful eye of the police and FBI, and the Patriot cell was more foolish and less dangerous than the cartels.

"Ah, well, I suppose. But you won't do it again?"

"The odds of my stumbling across a second band of terrorists are pretty small."

Not sharing that Special Agent Nichols had wondered if he might be open to more work, the consensus at the task force being that gardening was not a bad cover story for a confidential informant. Miguel was keeping the option on the table.

He promised he would be out to visit out West soon, and they disconnected.

Now, sipping his hot chocolate, Miguel Torres thought: of *course* he risked his life. He had to.

He would have helped the authorities bring them down, no matter what their plan. But he had a personal stake in Katherine's operation: the target that the cell had selected was none other than the Statue of Liberty, despised because she was a gift from a *foreign* country to America.

When he'd come to this country, he had not gotten his first sight of her from a ship, as had so many immigrants before him, but from the sky, as his airliner settled toward Newark airport on final approach from Mexico City.

It had been at that moment that he'd fallen in love with her and with everything she meant. She was why he often ate lunch here, why he occasionally strolled along these walkways even after a grueling day of work . . . simply so he could glance across the huge expanse of the Harbor for a glimpse of the majestic sculpture, which was, and would always be, the most important lady in his life.